CRITICAL PRAIRIE HEARTS

CAROLYN VACEY

Critical Prairie Hearts

All characters in this book are fictitious. Any resemblance to real persons, dead or alive, is purely coincidental

Tellwell Talent
www.tellwell.ca

ISBN
978-0-2288-5763-1 (Paperback)

DEDICATION

To my husband, Mike—my fortune cookie came true with you.

And to my daughters, Michaela, Annika, and Tatiana:

may you each find true love as I did.

CHAPTER 1

Code Blue

When Hayden reflected on that fateful beginning, she found it ironic that her heart was falling in love when someone else's heart was failing.

The night shift had started like any other in her job as a critical care nurse. General shift report in the staff break room began at 1900 hours. This was night shift number one of three on the rotation. Hayden's team all sat on the couches, fresh-faced for the night, but she knew by night number three, everyone would appear much wearier and less enthusiastic. There was general chitchat about what everyone did on their days off. Then it was time for the patient assignments to be read out by the nurse clinicians.

Hayden's nurse clinician, Peggy, read out everyone's assignment for the night in the Intensive Care Unit (ICU). Peggy was a fabulous and bright nurse and a wonderful clinician. She was a petite twenty-five-year-old with ringlets of thick chestnut brown hair that she wore in a ponytail. Her given name was Mary Margaret O'Reilly, true to her deeply Catholic Irish roots. She always wore a tiny gold cross around her neck, discreet under her scrubs. Peggy came from a wealthy family, and last year she married money: a geeky tall ophthalmologist named Eamon Fitzpatrick. Eamon's brother and Dad were both ophthalmologists, so it was expected that Eamon would be one, too. Peggy took her job as a clinician very seriously, but last month confessed to Hayden that she would just like to have some babies and stay at home.

"Ally, you will have room seven. Danni, you are going to be doubled with rooms eight and nine, and Hayden, you will be on codes and take the first admission in room twelve," Peggy instructed.

Danni was sitting next to Hayden and snorted when she heard her assignment. Hayden looked across the room to her friend Ally, who smirked and then rolled her eyes. Hayden looked away from Ally, as she knew if she made eye contact with her again, she would probably laugh out loud. Peggy finished reading out the staff assignment, and then everyone got up and proceeded into the ICU for their bedside report.

As Danni shuffled her plump body into the unit, she was mumbling under her breath, "I was just doubled last week. Some people get special treatment." Hayden ignored her, proceeded out of the break room, and almost ran into Betty, who was rushing in, late as usual. Betty was in her late fifties or early sixties. She was chronically late, always arriving like a tornado, out of breath, her hair astray, hauling in her backpack, lunch, and her coffee. Hayden chuckled, smiled, and said hello, and walked into the critical care hallway.

Hayden made her way into the ICU and headed towards the crash cart to complete her evening check. She checked the defibrillator and each drawer on the cart, ensuring that every medication and piece of potentially lifesaving equipment was accounted for. Hayden liked to be on the code team; it was exciting but a little nerve-wracking, rushing to any place in the hospital she may be called to and being part of the team to save someone's life. The code team consisted of two critical care nurses: one from the ICU and one from the Cardiac Intensive Care Unit (CCU), which was right across the hall from the ICU. At Calgary Memorial Hospital, the critical care nurses rotated, working between the ICU and the CCU. The code team also included a respiratory therapist, a nursing attendant to perform CPR, and a resident doctor from both the ICU and the CCU. During the day, the intensivist staff doctor may attend as well.

The ICU crash cart check was complete. Hayden noticed most everyone's bedside reports with the day shift staff were finishing up. Ally caught Hayden's eye from room seven's bedside and beckoned her over to her computer station.

"You know you have new residents on tonight, right?" Ally smiled sympathetically.

"Ohhhh, it is the first of the month!" Hayden groaned. New resident doctors started on the first day of the month, every three months. That often meant that they were unfamiliar with the ICU routines and could be less experienced, depending on where they were in their residency.

"I think you are lucky, though. I am pretty sure that one of them is Bernard Maplind, and I think he is quite smart. You know who I am talking about?" Ally smiled mischievously as she brushed her long auburn hair behind her ear.

Ally was Hayden's closest friend in the ICU. They had worked together on the same team now for two years and had supported each other. Hayden trusted her but at the same time knew that Ally *loved* to gossip.

"Is he the one that Louise is supposedly dating?" Hayden asked.

"Yes, and I think she is in CCU tonight and on codes with you!" Ally laughed. "Hey, can you come help me turn my patient? I have something else to tell you about Snorty over there." Ally lowered her voice and gestured with her chin towards Danni.

Hayden and Ally entered the patient's room. Each room in the ICU had sliding glass doors to enter. The room was filled with critical care equipment for the patient: the cardiac monitor displayed above the bed with multiple-colored lines and numbers, each reading an important vital sign. There was a ventilator breathing for the patient, several intravenous pumps infusing lifesaving medications, suction equipment, a feeding tube pump, sequential inflatable stockings, even the patient's bed was high tech. Each piece of equipment was essential for the patient's wellbeing. Critical care nurses must be familiar with every piece of equipment, its functionality and what each alarm means, sounds like, and how to troubleshoot it.

Hayden expertly and gently rolled Ally's patient, a frail seventy-two-year-old woman named Eunice, to her left side. They both explained out loud what they were doing, even though she was sedated and unconscious, both knowing that the patient could still hear them. It also warned Eunice what they were doing to alleviate any anxiety for the patient, despite her unconscious state. Ally listened to her lungs with her stethoscope and then gently rubbed Eunice's back with lotion. They repositioned her on her side, propped with pillows.

"She always complains. It does not matter what assignment she gets. And does the absolute minimal care for the patient. I don't know how she gets away with it," Ally lamented, referring to Danni. "Anyway, last week I was in the scheduling office and saw something on the desk addressed for her. Did you know her real name is *Dandelion*?"

"Seriously? Well, she once told me that her parents were hippies from Nelson, British Columbia, so I guess anything is possible." Hayden smiled and shook her head. The urgent beeping of her pager followed by the overhead announcement interrupted her thoughts and words.

"Code blue, unit fifty-seven, main building." Hayden didn't have to hear the second and third page; she swiftly headed for the code elevator. Ally was correct; Louise came breathlessly running up behind her just as the elevator doors were closing.

Louise was a petite blonde with large breasts and a big opinion. She loved being the center of attention. She had worked in ICU for only six months and frequently voiced her discontent that she had not been put in charge or that she did not get to care for the sickest patients. However, she seemed to respect Hayden and was always pleasant with her.

"Oh, I am glad it is you with me tonight, Hayden! I am such a black cloud when it comes to being on the code team! I am so excited because my *boyfriend,* Dr. Bernard Maplind, is on tonight. Did you know we were dating?" Louise prattled on, but Hayden was already focusing on her care ahead.

"I will take the patient if you can run the crash cart, okay, Louise?" Hayden directed as she exited the elevator and grabbed the crash cart parked outside the elevator. Richard, the nursing attendant, expertly steered it down the hall towards a nurse waving them down. She knew Louise would be right behind her.

Hayden entered the room to find three frantic-looking nurses, including one doing CPR on an elderly man. The respiratory therapist, Tim, had also just arrived and had begun bagging breaths into the patient. "Hi everyone, I am Hayden. This is Louise and Richard. What is happening?"

"He was just in the bathroom a few minutes ago, and then I came back to check on him and found him collapsed on the bed," relayed a nurse with the nametag 'Melanie.' Melanie appeared near tears.

"Could you tell us about his reason for admission and past medical history?" Hayden asked calmly as she was attaching the ECG leads from the monitor onto the patient's chest in preparation for assessing the patient's heart rhythm on the screen. Next was to establish another IV for medications. She expertly inserted a large-bore IV while Louise fumbled, putting on the defibrillation pads. Hayden patiently assisted her, then asked Richard to stop CPR so they could analyze the patient's heart rhythm and check for a pulse. Just as Hayden was observing the patient's heart rhythm on the monitor, she heard his voice as he entered the room.

"Hi, team. I am Jean Marc, and this is Bernie, your code physicians. What have we so far?" He looked directly at Hayden. For a split second, she was tongue-tied but then provided a concise report on the patient's collapse and care so far.

"The patient is in PEA (pulseless electrical activity), I've got Epinephrine 1 mg here drawn up, we have two IVs established, and Tim is on the airway," Hayden replied confidently.

The code ran so smoothly, and Hayden was in awe. Jean Marc made everyone in the room feel as though they were an important part of the team. He expertly and smoothly intubated the patient and never hesitated on what medications to order. He called Hayden by name when he requested a medication and again had that direct eye contact. He also listened and agreed when Hayden suggested inserting a gastric tube to decompress and remove the patient's gastric contents.

The man was successfully resuscitated, but his condition was tenuous. The team thanked the nurses on the floor as they urgently transferred the patient back down to the ICU, Hayden realizing this was her patient for the rest of her shift.

In the elevator, Jean Marc squished in next to Hayden. Tim, the respiratory therapist, was at the head of the bed bagging breaths into the patient's breathing tube, and Louise was there fussing with the IVs. Bernie was going to walk back to the CCU.

"Unfortunate to meet under these circumstances ladies, but Hayden and Louise, I look forward to working with you for the next couple months and having you direct poor old Bernie and me," Jean Marc smiled, again looking directly at Hayden. Although he was probably in his late twenties, he already had smile lines around his eyes.

"Oh my God, Jean Marc, it's not like we have not already met a million times! You and Bernie are housemates, after all!" Louise shrilled. Hayden ignored her and focused on her patient's vital signs and rhythm on the monitor. She was disappointed with Louise, who had fumbled with finding any equipment on the crash cart during the code and had been more of a hindrance than a helpful team member. Despite this, Hayden had been patient with her and helped her. She had been a new ICU nurse once and wanted to set an example as a mentor for Louise.

The night shift passed quickly as Hayden was so busy caring for her unstable patient, including titrating his intravenous medications to support his blood pressure and monitoring his other vital signs. Jean Marc spent most of the shift present or close by, giving orders for medications and then inserting a central line: a big intravenous in the patient's neck.

Hayden expertly organized all the equipment required for the procedure as Jean Marc donned his mask, sterile gown, and gloves.

"So, I thought Hayden was a boy's name? What's the deal?" Jean Marc teased as he set up his sterile tray.

"It was my mom's maiden name. My parents agreed to name me Hayden whether I was a boy or girl."

"I see," he surmised as he swabbed the patient's neck with sterile cleaning solution.

"So, I guess you are French?" Hayden smiled under her mask but could not look him directly in the eye.

Why can't you look him in the eye? Is this flirting? Is this appropriate while we are looking after this patient? This is so clichéd.

Her friends from home used to ask, "are there any cute doctors that you work with'? Is it just like those medical shows on TV?" Hayden used to laugh and roll her eyes. It's not like that at all! Many residents she worked with were married, were women, or were not anyone she would ever consider dating. Louise was a different story—she *wanted* to find and marry a doctor.

"Yes, my mom is French Canadian, but my dad was American, hence my last name of Garrison."

"How is it going in here?"

Hayden looked up to find Dr. Bernie Maplind standing in the doorway. Hayden had met him once before, and her encounter with him was pleasant. He was kind, patient, and obviously smart. Bernie, like Peggy's husband Eamon, came from a family of physicians. His dad, uncle, and sister were all physicians in the city.

"Bernie, my man, all is well! How is CCU tonight?" Jean Marc talked as he worked.

"Nice and quiet, since our code here. Good way to start the rotation!" Bernie smiled.

"Are you and Miss Louise behaving yourselves and not fraternizing on the job?" teased Jean Marc.

"Ah, none of that is going on, my friend!" Bernie blushed.

Hayden did not want to be unkind, but when she looked at Bernie, his head structure reminded her of Mr. Potato Head, a toy from her youth. *Although* she thought *he does not have a moustache. I am going straight to hell for thinking that.* He was not unattractive, just very plain….with a potato-shaped head.

As the two residents spoke, she drew off the morning lab work for her patient and primed an IV line for the big IV Jean Marc was inserting in her patient's neck.

"Hi, Hayden. Do you need any help?"

"Speak of the devil! Here she is!" Jean Marc joked. Hayden looked up to see Louise in the doorway, followed by Ally.

"Aren't you in CCU tonight, Louise? I can help Hayden. You should probably head back," Ally said, perhaps with a bit too much edge.

Louise gave Ally the death glare, squeezed Bernie's arm, and then left to return to CCU. Bernie followed her after mumbling a "Call me if you need me," to Jean Marc.

"Honestly, I don't know what he sees in her. He is such a nice guy," Ally sniped. Hayden shot her a look and silently shook her head 'no.' She didn't think that Ally realized that Bernie and Jean Marc were friends, let alone roommates.

"I do," Jean Marc snorted, insinuating it was the sex. All three burst out laughing, but Hayden felt guilty for gossiping.

Jean Marc completed the insertion of the line and was removing his sterile gown. "I think I will try and catch a few winks, ladies! I have taken all my sharps off the tray, Hayden. Page me if you need me," he said as he walked out the sliding glass door.

Ally and Hayden gently washed up her patient, changed his linens, and settled him. His vitals were now more stable. The shift was almost over, and Hayden was tired. As she cleaned up the equipment after the procedure, she looked out into the unit to see Danni sitting at her computer station, reading a book and eating her usual organic fruit gummies. She didn't go the extra mile for her patients.

"So, what do you think of doctor suave and debonair?" Ally asked as they finished straightening the mass of IV lines, snaking from the medication pumps and trailing down into the patient's veins.

"Who, Jean Marc?" Hayden replied. *Why did her stomach just flip-flop?*

"Yes! I can't say he is someone I would do a double-take on the street for, but there is something about him. He is so charming, and I love the wrinkles around his eyes."

"Yes, he is charming, but so was Ted Bundy. I am not interested in dating someone I work with, especially a doctor.

That is so cliché'." Hayden busied herself tidying her room as it was almost shift change and she had charting to finish.

"Sure, Jan!" Ally laughed as she walked out, referencing the *Brady Bunch* sisters.

Hayden gave her bedside report to the oncoming day shift nurse, Nancy. She was grateful she had everything in order because Nancy was known as 'No-Nonsense–Nancy,' a nickname Nancy knew existed, but she happily lived up to it. Her IV lines were always impeccably in order, everything labeled, and her patients were pristinely clean and comfortable. Your report had better be thorough, or she would be asking you a million questions. If you didn't have the answer, you would want to crawl under the computer desk.

Hayden drove home to her place and climbed gratefully into her bed. She was exhausted, but as she drifted off to sleep, the last thing that crossed her mind was those blue eyes and those smile lines.

CHAPTER 2

Dicentra Spectabilis

Hayden woke up at 3:20 p.m, surprised at how long she slept. She lived in a basement suite that had its own separate entrance in the back of the house. It was located in an older neighborhood in Calgary, but the homes were well-kept with manicured lawns and large established elm trees that canopied the streets. It was only a few blocks from the Bow River, and she frequently walked or rode her bike along the picturesque river pathway.

She opened her blackout blinds and squinted at the sun streaming in. The sky was cornflower blue and completely cloudless. Here it was a beautiful June day, and she was missing it. She wanted to go outside and enjoy some sunshine before her night shift tonight.

Even though it was a basement suite, the windows were large, and it didn't feel like a basement. Her suite was cozy. She had a small bedroom as well as a tiny den for an office. A coral-colored couch was the focal point in her living room, facing a television she rarely watched. There was a wicker shelf full of her favorite books and several thriving plants, their green vines trailing to the floor. Her kitchen and dinette space were small, but she was just cooking for herself. Her stomach growled as she looked in the fridge. She grabbed a raspberry yogurt and threw on her flip-flops, and headed up the stairs to the backyard. She opened the door as she heard a familiar bark.

"Hi, Finnegan! How is my favorite pup?" A small apricot-colored dog came bounding over to Hayden and licked her hand affectionately.

"Oh, my goodness, dear. I hope his barking didn't wake you!" Hayden looked up to see her landlord, Mrs. Rickleson, kneeling in one of her flowerbeds. She wore a floral kerchief on her head that held back her silver hair off her forehead.

"Not at all. I slept like a rock today. Your garden is looking so lovely, Lena."

Hayden's landlord, Lena Rickleson, was of German descent. She was widowed and spent her days baking for people in the neighborhood or working in her beautiful, impeccable garden. It was filled with multiple types of flowers and shrubs, and she also had a huge vegetable garden by August. Hayden was lucky to be the recipient of jams, pickles, and fresh veggies during the summer. Living here was like her home away from home.

"Come around here, Hayden. You must see the cherry tree at the side of the house. It is bursting with blooms, and the hum of the bees is amazing!"

Hayden stood under the pink blossoms and closed her eyes as she listened to the hum of the bees at work. It made her homesick, and she made a vow that she should be going home soon.

"You need some nourishment after working so hard all night. Let me wash up and grab you a freshly baked scone. I am done kneeling for today."

"Oh, Lena, that is okay. I have my yogurt here..." Hayden knew it was futile to refuse food from Lena. If you said you were full, she would insist you needed more.

"I need to go check the roast anyway. Lawrence is coming for dinner and is bringing a friend. I am not sure if it will be a lady friend, but I am making a nice spread for them." Lena chattered as she went in the back door, wiping her hands on her gardening apron.

Hayden chuckled to herself. Lawrence, or Larry as he told Hayden he preferred to be called, was clearly gay but Lena did not want to seem to accept that. She was always talking about Lawrence bringing home a lady friend, but if it turned out to be a man, then she would say he was a "work friend."

She threw a ball for Finnegan, who gratefully ran to fetch it. Hayden walked around the garden, admiring the pink tulips and yellow daffodils in full bloom. The green lines of sprouts in the vegetable garden peeked through the rich dark soil: carrots, peas, onions, potatoes, lettuce, and beets. The empty seed packages placed overtop wooden stakes marked the beginning of each row. But Hayden didn't need to read the stakes. She knew each plant from her parents' expansive garden at home in the summer.

She kicked off her flip-flops and walked barefoot in the lush green grass, appreciating the cool, spongy consistency. As she stood there, the distinct fragrance of lilacs floated over. Hayden peeked around the back garage and saw the lilac tree was loaded with blossoms. How had she missed that this morning when she drove home? Snapping off some stems, she knew the blossoms would fill her suite with their intoxicating aroma.

She threw the ball again for Finnegan, who was patiently panting by her side. She walked over to another part of the garden, where bright purple hyacinth and crocuses popped from their green bases in the soil. Then, in a partially shady area of the yard, she looked at her favorite plant, a *dicentra spectabilis* or bleeding heart. It was laden with little pink hearts. Hayden's mind drifted....hearts....that need restarting. Her mind went back to the code blue from last night and then to Jean Marc. *Really? Why did he make an impact on her?*

"Hayden? I have your scone here for you."

Her mind snapped back to reality. "Thank you so much, Lena, that is so kind of you. I hope you don't mind that I took some lilacs, they are so fragrant, and they remind me of home."

"Of course not, dear, please help yourself." Lena smiled.

"Listen, I will get Finnegan out for a long walk sometime soon, okay?" Hayden would often take Finnegan for long walks along the river pathway on her days off. "I need to get going and shower before work. Thanks again!"

Back in her suite, Hayden had a long luxurious shower and stepped out onto the pink bathmat. She gave herself a once-over in the mirror as she slathered lotion on her long legs.

"*Long legs like these are a jockey's dream*!" She closed her eyes and pushed the memory away.

Hayden was tall at five foot ten and with a slim build. She had played on her high school basketball team and ran for varsity track, but she didn't run anymore. Growing up, she had also kept in shape by helping on the farm; she never backed down from any chores or helping her dad. Now, at twenty-five years old, her routine was brisk walks in the neighborhood, and she had weights that she exercised with on her yoga mat three times a week.

She ran a brush through her thick, long chestnut hair. Hayden frequently had comments from girls who were envious of her hair. In the summer, she would often have streaks of gold in it from the sun. As she blew dry her locks, she examined her face closer in the mirror. She was having luck with a new skin care routine in the last few months. She had struggled with acne in early high school, and even now, she had the occasional breakouts.

Hair up in a ponytail, a quick application of mascara to her green eyes, and into her scrubs, Hayden was almost ready for her shift. She made her lunch and then checked her texts. There was one from her mom, giving her the latest update on the farm, and another from her friend Clairese, a nurse who worked in emergency at Memorial Hospital.

"We need to go for drinks! I've got lots to tell you, Coyote!"

Hayden smiled at the reference. Three years back, Clairese and Hayden had met at the Memorial Hospital general orientation when they were both hired as new nurses. They had become fast friends and went out socially, especially that first year. Clairese was a firecracker—very outspoken and the life of any party, especially if there were attractive men around. Last summer, they had been at a Calgary Stampede event with colleagues from emergency, ICU/CCU and EMS. Clairese had consumed a lot of alcohol and was telling a group of guys some jokes and funny stories.

"Have you met my friend here, Hayden? She is SINGLE, guys! I know, it is hard to believe that this cutie is single, but here she is!" Clairese kept calling her cutie all night, but in her intoxicated state, it came out as 'cah-yootie.' Hayden went home early that night, and when she spoke to Clairese the next day, she asked her why she kept calling her Coyote all night. They both howled with laughter when they realized the mispronunciation, and the nickname stuck.

Hayden looked at her watch and realized she had better head to the hospital. She was habitually early. She liked to relax before her shift started. Locking her door, she walked towards the back garage to get in her car. Just as she reached for the door handle of the side door to enter the garage, the door opened. Startled, Hayden jumped back to see Larry in the garage.

"Oh, hi, just leaving for work?" Larry never addressed Hayden by her name. She wasn't sure if he had forgotten her name or what the deal was.

"Um, yes, just heading out." Hayden stepped back to allow Larry into the yard. Another man, dressed in jeans and a tight red tank top, followed behind him. He had black curly hair with some threads of grey, tiny gold hoop earrings, and several tattoos on his arms.

"Oh, this is my friend, Jezz." Larry gushed. "We are having dinner with Mom."

No introduction was made of her, and Jezz stared back at Hayden with dark eyes. There was an awkward pause.

"Oh, I'm Hayden. I live downstairs." Hayden reluctantly put her hand out, and Jezz grasped just the end of Hayden's fingers and gave them a brief, cold shake.

"Interesting," was all Jezz replied. Hayden suddenly felt uncomfortable, and much to her dismay, the hair stood up on the back of her neck. She pulled her hand away quickly.

"Well, I must get going. Have a great dinner!" Hayden moved towards the garage, but in her rush, she dropped her lunch bag. Larry and Jezz walked to the back entrance of the house. As she gathered her lunch bag, she looked back to the house—Jezz was staring back at her. She stepped into the garage. *What a fucking creep,* she thought.

The uneasy feeling started to dissipate by the time she reached the turn-off to the hospital. Her focus was now on her shift ahead as she maneuvered her car towards the staff parking in front of the hospital.

Calgary Memorial is a huge teaching hospital. It is centrally situated in the city, minutes from downtown, which is just across the river. The multi-building complex of Calgary Memorial is located on a main thoroughfare, so it has easy access to the ring road surrounding the city. It is a Level One Trauma Center for the city of Calgary and is a well-respected facility.

Hayden parked her car in the staff parking lot and headed towards the main entrance. Blossoming trees surrounded the front of the hospital, and their sweet evening fragrance was perceptible. Just before reaching the hospital entrance, Hayden heard the familiar and distinctive low rumble and knew that STARS rescue helicopter was en route. She paused, looking up to the sky, and watched as the characteristic red helicopter approached the hospital. It passed over the hospital to the landing pad at the back, which linked directly into the emergency department. *Someone is bleeding from a trauma, or someone's heart has stopped,* she thought. *Bleeding hearts...*Hayden's mind raced between Lena's garden of flowers, the uncomfortable encounter with Jezz, her code blue last night, and Jean Marc.

I need to focus, she thought. *I think it is going to be a busy night.*

Hayden opened the hospital door and headed up to the critical care unit, not knowing what was in store for her.

CHAPTER 3

Dating Apps

When Hayden entered the staff locker room, there was lots of chatter as her colleagues readied for their shift.

"Hayden, you're here!" exclaimed the first voice of the group.

"I bet you are so happy to see us!"

Hayden *was* happy to see these two colleagues, Alana and Shaye. They were part of her team and were both excellent nurses. The two were best friends, roommates, travel companions, and did everything together, including dating the same pool of men. Hayden wasn't sure how their friendship hadn't imploded at some point.

The girls each embraced Hayden. They had just returned from a month-long trip to Thailand and appeared tan and rejuvenated.

"We just heard about the new dreamy resident and how he has the hots for you!" gushed Alana.

"What? Who told you that?" demanded Hayden. "That is not true!"

"Danni did!" they both said in unison.

Incredulously, Hayden looked over at Danni. Danni's expression was flat like it always was, but then she smiled thinly.

"It was evident watching him last night in your patient's room, the way he looked at you." Danni scorned.

Hayden felt her face flush. "I think you are all reading into nothing. I don't think he is interested in me. He was just being friendly on his first shift. Besides, I am not Louise and interested in dating a doctor!"

The locker room fell silent, and Hayden already knew before looking that Louise must have entered and was behind her. Hayden turned to find Louise standing there with her arms folded, clearly displeased.

"I just came in to tell you, Hayden, that Peggy is sick for tonight. Capathia asked me to find you and tell you that you are in charge of CCU tonight." With that, Louise turned on her heels and walked out.

"Oh, okay," stammered Hayden, but the door had already shut.

Alana and Shaye suppressed giggles. Danni did not look at Hayden and walked out.

"Great," Hayden said sarcastically as she put her belongings in her locker.

"Don't worry about it," reassured Shaye, "she'll get over it!"

"Get over what?" asked Ally as she came into the locker room.

"We'll fill you in. It's about Louise." Shaye replied. "Hayden is in charge, so she has to go."

Hayden headed into the break room to meet up with the day shift clinician, Capathia Reynolds. Capathia was a large African American lady with a booming laugh. She moved to Calgary from the southern United States after marrying a Canadian man. She had worked as a clinician in ICU and CCU for many years and was very knowledgeable. Capathia ran a tight ship and had high expectations of her nurses. However, she was the first to lend a hand to her staff, and she was so compassionate with grieving families. Hayden had great respect for her.

"Hello girl, I hope y'all don't mind I put you in charge. Peggy is gone sick tonight, but between you and me, I think she has a pea in the pod, and that's what's makin' her green!"

"Oh, that would be great if she was pregnant!" smiled Hayden.

Hayden looked down to see her staff assignment sheet and remembered that Louise worked in CCU last night, so she would be with her tonight. She sighed. This was going to be awkward.

There were about twelve permanent nurses on Hayden's team. The rest of the shift team was comprised of part-time or casual nurses. Besides the nurse clinicians, four nurses usually worked in the CCU, and the rest of the team were in the ICU for the shift.

Hayden read out the assignments, received a unit report from Capathia, and then headed into the CCU to check in at each bedside. She took a deep breath when she reached the rooms where Louise was the assigned nurse.

Louise gave her a brief, curt update on her three assigned patients, followed by an awkward pause.

"Look, Louise, I am sorry about what I said in the locker room. I did not mean to offend you," Hayden said sincerely.

"None taken. I know most people are jealous that Bernie and I are dating. So, what if I want to marry a doctor? I will be happy, and everyone else can be miserable, dating losers on dating apps." Louise looked triumphant.

"Well, I am not sure…" Hayden began and then thought, *this is a futile conversation.* "Anyway, I am glad you are not offended."

"But Hayden, just so you know, I was at Bernie and Jean Marc's place this afternoon, and Jean Marc asked me about you."

Hayden's stomach flip-flopped. "Oh, is that right?"

"Just think if you two got involved, we could double date or do dinners together!" Louise clasped her hands together and smiled.

"Well, I need to get to the other rooms. Uh, thanks for the update." Hayden left and went to check in with the other nurses. She was unsure how she felt about Louise's comment.

The night shift was thankfully not busy in CCU, so it left a lot of time for Hayden to think. She reflected on her last 'relationship' of three months, which was last year. After encouragement from Ally, Hayden gave in and had tried a dating app. Louise was kind of right; he did turn out to be a loser. Well, maybe not at first.

Kevin Clark was a twenty-eight-year-old police officer with the city. He had not revealed that on the dating app, understandably. They had a few text and phone conversations before they agreed to meet up on their first date at a Starbucks. Kevin was her height, but a very muscular build with a thick neck, as he worked out frequently. He was blond but was losing his hair, so had it cropped short. Hayden was happy to meet someplace public in case she needed an escape plan. He stood when she walked into the coffee shop.

"Hayden?" he smiled. Nice smile, crooked teeth. *Give him a chance, Hayden*!

"Hi, Kevin!" she extended her hand. Good firm handshake. Her dad always said that was a good sign.

"Whew, I am glad you didn't lie on your driver's license! I can't tell you how many people lie about their height and weight. You are right on!" he smiled appreciatively as he gave her a once over.

He checked my weight and height on my driver's license?! Alarm bells went off in Hayden's head. Her face must have indicated that as Kevin immediately began to stammer.

"I mean, I am sorry, but I am a police officer and… I am sorry, I just need to make sure…there are so many crazies out there." He appeared embarrassed.

"Okay, I guess I understand." Hayden removed her coat and sat down. Kevin looked relieved and joined her at the table.

The date proceeded better, and they actually had an engaging conversation. Hayden decided to let the weight and height checkup go and give him a chance. At the end of the afternoon, he asked if they could meet again. He hugged her goodbye and kissed her on the cheek.

"Give him a chance!" Ally encouraged her after Hayden relayed her first date experience with Kevin. "You need to go on some dates, Hayden, and move on." Ally's words stung. *She had moved on, hadn't she*?

"Go have some fun, get out of the house. Maybe have some casual sex, no strings attached!" Ally laughed.

"Ally! I am not into that. That is how you get an STI," Hayden scoffed.

Her second date with Kevin was good. She allowed him to pick her up (he was a cop after all), and he even brought her flowers (Safeway blue-dyed daisies, but the thought was there).

"This is a peace offering for the weight and height checkup." Kevin chuckled as he handed them to her.

Dating a police officer was challenging as they both worked shifts, so it was sometimes hard to line up their schedules. But after a month, Kevin asked the question.

"So, I was wondering if we could be exclusive?"

Hayden was not sure if she wanted to be in a committed relationship quite yet. Or was it that she was not sure if she wanted to be in a relationship *with Kevin*? She liked Kevin, but there were some inkling doubts at the back of her mind. He texted her frequently, always wanting to know what she was doing and with who.

Despite that, she enjoyed his company, and truthfully, she did not want to be alone. *Because when you are lonely, you know your thoughts go back in time, and that is too painful, isn't it, Hayden*?

Two months into the 'exclusivity' with Kevin, she regretted her decision. She had been invited to Shaye and Alana's place for a movie night with some of the girls from work. Kevin did not want her to go.

"What's the problem?" she asked him on the phone.

"Those girls are a bit wild. I don't really like you hanging around them. Besides, I am going to be off at 2300 and thought I could stop by for a little cuddle." He whispered the last few words into the phone. *Why had she slept with him*? Regret, regret, regret. And to make matters worse, he was also insinuating that he was falling in love with her. She was not anywhere near those feelings.

Despite his reservations, Hayden went to the movie night, but she had a sick feeling in the pit of her stomach all evening. She did not tell anyone her predicament, mostly because she knew what they would say. She ignored his multiple texts, but then she feigned illness and went home at 11:15. As she drove down the alley to pull into the garage, she was alarmed but not entirely surprised to see Kevin's jeep parked at the end of the alley.

As she closed the garage and walked into the yard, she heard the jeep's door shut. Her heart was in her throat.

"Hi, Babe!" Kevin called over the fence. "Home from the hen party so soon?" She hated him calling her 'babe.'

"Kevin, what are you doing?" Suddenly, she felt assertive.

"I just wanted to see you. What's wrong with that?" Kevin had opened the gate and came into the yard.

Hayden knew that Lena would not hear them in the yard, but she lowered her voice.

"Look, Kevin, I just don't think this is going to work between us. You just seem to have different expectations for this relationship. And unfortunately, I am just not on the same plane as you. I'm sorry." Hayden shivered.

Kevin stood in silence for a minute, his silhouette in the dark. He sighed and then, to Hayden's surprise, replied softly, "I was kind of picking up on that these last few days. I really like you, Hayden, but I get what you are saying."

They stood in awkward silence. It was cold out, and Hayden just wanted to go into her warm bed and go to sleep.

"Can I give you a hug goodbye?" he asked.

Hayden was hesitant, then walked over and hugged him. She let go quickly. "I am sorry, Kevin." She quickly retreated into her suite. She peeked out her blinds, but he was gone. Then she heard the jeep drive away.

Hayden was surprised when hot tears trickled on her pillow. She knew the tears weren't for Kevin. The tears were because of endings. *Sometimes endings happen because you end them, but sometimes they happen out of your control.*

Hayden fell asleep, her heart broken all over again.

CHAPTER 4

Breakfast Beginnings

The rest of Hayden's night shift in CCU was uneventful, and she went home but slept poorly. She woke up at around 2:30 in the afternoon and lay in bed until three. She texted Clairese back and then called her mom.

"Hayden! I am so glad to hear from you! Have you been working too hard?" her mom exclaimed.

Hayden explained she was on a stretch of nights but that she was still planning to come home tomorrow for her days off. Her mom was thrilled and said she would make her favorite supper for her.

"Dad and Paddy will be happy to see you, too!" she assured Hayden.

Paddy was Hayden's brother, who was seven years younger. Hayden's mom, Winnie, had suffered multiple miscarriages between Hayden and her brother Patrick's birth. Patrick was a big help on the family farm to their dad, Cedric, who everyone called Ced.

Hayden reluctantly crawled out of her bed and lifted her blind. It was grey and cool out with a summer rainstorm. A big change from yesterday, but that was Calgary's weather. The saying goes, if you don't like the weather in Calgary, wait five minutes.

She showered and got ready and then headed to work for night shift number three. As predicted, the chatter was quieter in the break room before the shift started, as everyone was tired.

Ally came in and sat down next to her. "Hey, I never got to talk to you last night after the locker room incident. What happened with Louise?" she asked quietly.

"Nothing really. I apologized, and Louise said that she and Bernie would be happy, and we would all be miserable on dating apps." Hayden looked at Ally, and they both chuckled.

"Well, I guess she is not really wrong," Ally replied.

Carl was the clinician for CCU tonight. He was a tall, lanky forty-five-year-old ex-military nurse with thinning black hair and was a heavy smoker. He had been a clinician for a long time, and while he was good at his job, he was often intimidating to new staff and had earned the nickname 'Snarl.' Hayden was always happier when she was working in the unit that Peggy was overseeing. While she had never had a problem with Carl, and he was always pleasant with her, she didn't respect Carl's approach with things.

Thankfully, Hayden was in ICU tonight, and Peggy had returned. Peggy looked tired and maybe a bit queasy. Maybe Capathia was right about her. She was reading out the patient assignments.

"Danni, you have room one, and the patient is coming back from the OR. Alana rooms two and three; Shaye room four; Hayden room five. Louise, STARS is bringing in an ICU transfer from Red Deer, who is septic, and you will have them in room six. Ally, you will be floating and can help Louise."

Peggy continued reading out the rest of the assignment for the ICU, but Hayden was looking over at Louise who had a smile of satisfaction on her face with her assignment. Hayden wondered which residents were on duty tonight.

Hayden's patient was a sixty-four-year-old man who was postoperative day two from some orthopedic surgeries after being in a motor vehicle collision. He was sedated and very stable. She completed her thorough head-to-toe assessment and then decided to look for Richard, the nursing attendant, to help her turn her patient. As she stepped outside her room, she saw Jean Marc enter the other end of the unit. Jean Marc was about six feet tall with a slim build and strawberry blond hair. As Ally said, he was not drop-dead gorgeous, but he had this *swagger* when he walked.

What made him so intriguing? When he spoke to you, he engaged you like there was no one else he would rather talk to. Then there were those blue eyes, which, at that very moment, looked up to find her staring. He smiled, and Hayden smiled back, then she quickly looked away, grateful when she saw Richard.

After turning and settling her patient, she sat down at her computer, just outside the sliding glass door, to complete her charting and document her patient assessment. She looked over to see Danni discussing her patient with Jean Marc, and she did not appear happy. Her patient, Merle, had been a patient on the unit for several weeks. He was being weaned off the ventilator and was frequently agitated. He was aptly but inappropriately nicknamed 'Merle the Squirrel' because of it. He often pinched nurses during care or had his hands in his incontinence pad, despite having soft restraints on his wrists. Danni was not happy with Jean Marc's order not to give Merle any sedation for the evening.

"Louise, STARS is landing with your patient in five minutes, and they will be bringing him directly up here since it is an ICU-to-ICU transfer," Peggy informed Louise.

"If you need my help, Louise, I am here as well," offered Hayden. She wondered how the dynamic would be with Ally and Louise working together.

Hayden had just finished her charting when the STARS crew walked in with the patient on the helicopter stretcher. He was attached to a portable cardiac monitor, and they were bagging breaths into the patient's endotracheal tube. The two crew members were wearing their distinctive blue flight suits, but they had removed their helmets.

"Hey, you two!" Hayden greeted. The flight nurse was Scarlett, who worked in the ICU on a different team, and the paramedic was Hudson Cooper, who everyone called "Coop." The two had met while working at STARS and had married this past November up in Banff. Hayden had attended the wedding and really liked the couple.

They only had a few moments to give their report to the ICU receiving team before their radios went off, dispatching them to another call.

"We'll have to catch up another time, Lady!" Scarlett called to Hayden as they rolled their empty stretcher out the ICU door, rushing back down to emergency to access the helicopter pad. Hayden could hear the whirring of the helicopter blades starting up. She got up from her seat and went to the ICU window, which looked directly down to the helicopter pad. She watched Coop load the stretcher into the back of the helicopter and Scarlett get in the side door. Hayden knew it would be an exciting job as a flight nurse. Scarlett had shared many stories about her calls. However, she also knew she did not have the stomach to fly in a small helicopter. *And maybe going to a motor vehicle scene call might be too traumatizing, right, Hayden?* She pushed that thought away and went back to her workstation.

Hayden poked her head in periodically next door and saw that Louise and Ally were working together well. Louise's face was flushed with excitement as she assessed and monitored her critical patient and titrated lifesaving medications for them. Hayden looked down the ICU hallway at Danni, who did not appear happy with her agitated patient. Having to go in his room off and on most of the night, she could not sit at her computer and read or do her crossword puzzles, something that Hayden would never do on any downtime as an ICU nurse.

Louise went for her coffee break, and Ally was relieving her. Ally suddenly called Hayden over.

"His blood pressure is dropping, and he is having more PVCS." (Premature ventricular contractions, which were abnormal beats of the heart), "Can you call Jean Marc in?" Ally's face appeared worried.

Hayden asked Gurpreet, the unit clerk, to page both Jean Marc and Peggy and then went in to help Ally. "Do you want me to call Louise back?"

"No, she needs a break," Ally said genuinely. "She has actually done quite well in here tonight."

Jean Marc arrived in a minute and had obviously had his head down for a rest—his hair was astray on one side, and he had a crease on his cheek where he had laid. But he smiled at Hayden when he walked in.

"What is happening, ladies?" he questioned with genuine concern.

After giving the patient some intravenous fluid boluses that Jean Marc ordered and titrating his intravenous medications, Ally and Hayden stabilized the patient. They sent off blood work to check the patient's electrolytes as well.

Peggy, the nurse clinician, came by the room. "Sorry, I was helping Danni in room one. I am glad this guy is more stable. His family should be arriving soon."

Jean Marc was sitting outside the room, looking through the chart. "I am not very popular on that end of the unit tonight," he gestured towards Danni's patient in room one. "Hopefully, my humble orders down here were satisfactory to you ladies."

Peggy gave Jean Marc a side-eyed look with a smirk. "I am going to check on some other people now. Call me back if you need anything, Ally and Hayden."

Hayden and Jean Marc chatted for about twenty minutes. This time, *he* seemed mesmerized by what Hayden said instead of the other way around. Just then, Shaye walked over, followed by Louise returning from her break.

"Hey everyone," Shaye smiled, "who is up for breakfast at *Bro'kin Yolk* after the shift?"

"Oh, I am for sure!" Louise chirped, "Bernie would love to join us too. He is on in CCU tonight."

Jean Marc looked directly at Hayden. "Are you up for it? Sounds fun."

Hayden wasn't sure if it was her heart or her stomach that flipped, but she was definitely up for it.

"I'm in," she answered enthusiastically.

The rain had dissipated overnight, and the sun was up when they all met at the restaurant after their shift. Bernie and Jean Marc came later as they had to complete mini rounds with the oncoming residents in the morning. Louise waited to drive with Bernie. Danni was still angry from dealing with Merle the Squirrel all night, so she declined. Peggy and others on the team were too tired, so it was a small group.

"How did it go with Louise last night, Ally?" Shaye inquired as she squeezed honey in her tea.

"It was actually not that bad. She was too busy to boast and carry on, but I am sure we will hear it all this morning!" Ally sipped her coffee.

"You have great patience," Alana began, "she is so full of herself sometimes." She leaned forward in a conspiring manner and lowered her voice. "You know, my friend Chloe went to nursing school with her. They used to call her Sealy."

"Sealy?" they all inquired in unison.

"You know, Sealy Posturepedic…a mattress? She was always on her back sleeping around."

They all burst out laughing, but Hayden felt a bit guilty for gossiping again. Ally relished in it.

Bernie, Jean Marc, and Louise arrived shortly after, and it ended up being such a fun time with them all. There were lots of laughs and the occasional 'dark humor' comment, as it can go for health care workers.

Jean Marc had sat across from Hayden, and several times during the morning, she caught him staring.

The caffeine was wearing off, and suddenly, Hayden felt tired. She looked at her watch and was shocked to see it was 11:45 a.m.

"I need to go and get some sleep, guys! This has been fun!" Almost in unison, everyone murmured the same thing. The bill was settled, and the group scattered to the parking lot, hollering goodbyes.

Hayden walked towards her car, aware that Jean Marc was behind her. Suddenly, they were the only ones around.

"What, no truck?" he teased.

"Why do you think I would drive a truck?" she laughed.

"Louise tells me you are a country farm girl." He smiled, his eyes twinkling, even in his tired state.

So, he was *asking about me.*

"Well, I am a city girl now, so I drive a car." She unlocked her car with the fob and smiled back, not afraid anymore to make direct eye contact with him. She leaned back against the driver's door.

"Sporty." He nodded approvingly at her blue Honda civic, although it was six years old but still in good shape.

"What do you drive?" she asked, raising her eyebrows.

"I have my trusty SUV." He motioned over to an older red bronco, two parking spaces down. "I'm not like my buddy Bernie with Daddy's money, driving a Range Rover!"

"I see," she said, smiling. *Another attraction for Louise: money.*

"Well, I am driving home to my parents' later today, so I need to get some sleep. This was fun!" Hayden opened her vehicle door.

"Can I text you on your days off? Maybe we can go for our own breakfast sometime?"

She blushed inexplicably, tucking her hair behind one ear. They exchanged numbers, and then Hayden smiled and said goodbye.

Driving back to her place, she suddenly wasn't so sure she would be able to sleep before her drive back to the farm.

CHAPTER 5

Small Town Country Girl

Despite her exciting morning, Hayden was able to sleep for the afternoon. She woke with a start at 4:30 p.m. She was upset she had slept so long as she still needed to run some errands before her drive to the farm. She would not be there in time for supper. She texted her mom with a request to keep her supper warm, but she would be there closer to six-thirty.

She quickly showered and packed her bag. As she came out the back door, Lena was hanging some clothes on a little clothesline, something Hayden's mom still did. Clothes always smelled so fresh after that.

"Hi, Lena. I am just on my way out to my parents for a day or so. I will be home on Tuesday, and if it is nice, I will take Finnegan for a walk."

"Okay, dear, not to worry. Please drive safe." Lena said, clipping the clothes on the line with her wooden clothespins.

Hayden hesitated for a moment. Lena did not seem herself; there was a certain sadness about her.

"Is everything okay?" Hayden inquired in concern.

"Yes, Hayden, all is fine. Say hello to your folks and give Paddy a big hug for me." She smiled half-heartedly and then turned to hang more clothes.

Hayden wavered and then decided she should get on the road. The sky had black clouds looming in the south.

"I will, Lena. Have a good few days." Hayden headed to the garage and got on the road.

Was Lena upset she hadn't walked Finnegan? She doubted that, as it had never been an issue before. Was it her dinner with Larry and creepy Jezz? She decided that she would make an effort with Lena when she got home, have a tea, and spend some time with her. Maybe she would open up.

Fortuitously, rush hour traffic leaving the city was not that bad, and soon enough, she was on the highway driving south. Her hometown of Willow Creek was about eighty minutes south of Calgary, and her farm about ten minutes from town.

The rain from yesterday had greened up the landscape beautifully. The crops were lush for the end of June. She knew what each type of field would yield as she passed by them; her dad had taught her well. This part of the country grew a lot of wheat and canola. She knew in a month that the expansive canola fields would be a brilliant yellow. She cracked her window open and inhaled the sweet country air.

As her car rolled south, those black clouds descended towards her. It could be hail, but she hoped for the farmers' sake it would only be heavy rain. She could feel the air become dense, even being inside the vehicle. The sun had retreated, and despite only being close to 6:00 p.m, the sky was dark.

The clouds opened up with rain just as Hayden took the turn off to the secondary highway to lead her to Willow Creek. She had driven this route so many times that she could probably do it with her eyes closed. The heavy rain in front of her almost imitated that.

Willow Creek is a small agricultural town in the foothills of southern Alberta. The creek loops lazily through the picturesque town and eventually intersects and joins the Oldman River much farther south. Main Street has many old historic brick and sandstone buildings and was the backdrop for two movies. Tree-lined streets with charming front porch houses stretched for several blocks each way. Red brick or white clapboard churches dotted the corners. Despite now living in the city, Hayden is proud to say this is her hometown. The town has a vibrant population built on the foundation of hard work, family, and community.

Hayden barely could see the highway sign indicating Willow Creek was two kilometers away due to the rain pounding on her windshield. She slowed down, knowing what was ahead on her left without even looking: the wrought iron fence, the willow and poplar trees, and the cotoneaster hedge. She took a deep breath and focused her eyes on her drive ahead.

Five minutes later, the large colorful sign welcomed her to the town of Willow Creek. Main Street was deserted, but as she turned off on Railway Street, she saw that *Andy's Diner and Pub* was packed; the parking lot was full with pick-up trucks. *Some things never change.* She smiled.

Leaving town, she drove over the train tracks, then onto her favorite quaint wooden bridge over the creek, and soon reached her Range Road. The rain had let up, and despite being well-experienced driving on gravel, she proceeded a bit slower on the road. Barbed wire fences lined both sides of the road, and she could see the occasional hawk perched on a pole, predatory watching for a potential meal. As she approached the next Range Road intersection, a group of starlings swooped majestically in the field.

Turning onto the next Range Road, she sped up a bit, anticipating her arrival home. She could see the grey roof of her house behind the large grove of trees ahead. She slowed and saw the wooden welcome sign: *Barrett Ranch: Ced, Winnie, Hayden, and Patrick.*

She pulled into the drive, which was lined on both sides with large trees. At the clearing, the family home was on the left, the four-door garage straight ahead and the red barn tucked further back on the right.

Her family home was a blue and white two-story, with a large front wrap-around porch. Her dad and mom had inherited the farm from her dad's parents. She knew deep down that her dad worried about what would happen to the farm in the upcoming years, but he never brought it up with Hayden.

She saw her mom and Paddy waving from the kitchen window. Butch, the black lab family dog, came running to greet Hayden. His feet were muddy, but she didn't care.

"Hi, my Butch! You dirty mess!" Butch's tail wagged appreciatively as she patted him on the behind. Hayden had not noted the grey in his muzzle last time she was home. *When was the last time she was home?*

She climbed the porch just as her mom opened the screen door.

"Well, you are a sight for sore eyes!" her mom exclaimed with open arms.

"Hi, Mom." Hayden smiled as she gave her a big hug. "Mmmm, supper smells so good!"

Her brother Patrick was right behind with another hug. "Hi, Sister!"

"Did you grow taller since I saw you last? You seem taller, Paddy!" Hayden exclaimed.

Paddy smiled shyly. "I don't know."

"We waited to have a late supper with you. Dad will be in anytime soon. He is out checking on a calf."

The Barretts ran a cattle ranch, as had her grandparents before them. They usually had around 150 head, and now with spring, there were a lot more with new calves.

"Come sit down and have a few veggies and dip. I am going to pull the chicken potpie out of the oven now; it should be ready. Paddy, why don't you get your sister a drink and then go and call your dad in for dinner."

"Mom, I am fine. I can get my own drink. I am sure Dad heard me pull in."

Despite Hayden's protest, Paddy went out the back porch door to look for and call for Ced.

Hayden sat at the table and savored the smell coming from the kitchen. Her mom had come through with her promise to make Hayden's favorite dinner. She munched on some carrots while her mom chattered about the latest news in town: Mrs. Scott, an elderly neighbor was sick in the hospital; 'the Callahan girl' from a few farms over was dating 'the oldest Dickson boy' from town; and Mrs. McDowell, a former teacher of Hayden's was supposedly getting a divorce.

"What is new with you, Hayden?" her mom inquired as she added chopped tomatoes into a salad. Hayden knew indirectly that her mom was really asking if she was seeing anyone.

"Not much, Mom. Just working," she replied as she sipped her water.

"Have you been in touch with Shelby lately?"

Hayden lowered her eyes as she knew this question had been coming. "No, I haven't," she said quietly.

Winnie stopped tossing the salad, lowered her head, and looked disappointedly at her. "Hayden…"

"I know, I know. But I am sure she is busy with the girls," Hayden pleaded.

Shelby was her best friend from high school and had gotten married shortly after graduation to a rodeo cowboy named Dean Winchester. They had dated each other all through school. Two months ago, Shelby gave birth to twin daughters, Haven and Hadley. After their birth, Hayden visited them and attended a baby shower for Shelby before they were born. She felt guilty that she had not been more in touch.

"I know that Tate and June have been giving them lots of help, but June still has challenges after her stroke," Winnie sighed.

"It's still so hard, Mom…" Hayden began but was interrupted by the back porch door opening.

"Daddy's here!" grinned Paddy as he entered, followed behind by Hayden's dad, Ced.

"Hi, Dad!" Hayden got up to hug her father.

"Good to have you home, Bunny!" Her dad said, referring to her by her childhood nickname, and he reciprocated the warm hug. "Supper smells great. I am starved."

It felt wonderful to sit down with her family for a meal. They played a game of cards after dinner, and then Hayden decided to turn in early. She hadn't slept enough today after her night shift. She hugged everyone good night and crawled into her childhood single bed under a homemade patchwork quilt. As she lay there, the guilt of her not visiting home enough and her conversation about Shelby sat like a stone in her stomach. She drifted off to sleep and dreamt of her childhood: swinging in the poplar tree tire swings and hanging out in the hayloft with Shelby. And, she dreamt of ladybugs.

CHAPTER 6

Trip into Town

Hayden awoke to her phone buzzing. At first, she was confused about where she was, then the sleep haze cleared, and she picked up her phone. There was a text from Jean Marc.

I hope you are having fun at the farm! If you are back early, text me so we can go for breakfast or lunch. JM ☺

Should she text him back right away? She decided to wait a while. She lay back down on the bed. She could hear the gator (a small all-terrain vehicle) driving around outside, so she knew her dad and Paddy would be up doing chores. The smell of coffee floated up the stairs.

Hayden took a deep breath and called Shelby. It went to voicemail after four rings.

"Hey, Shelb. I am so sorry I have not been in closer touch. I have been working lots and just drove down last night to see the family. If you are up for a visitor, call me back, and I can drive out to see you. Miss you! Give those babies a kiss and Dean a hug." She breathed a sigh of relief that she had at least called and left a message.

After her shower, she headed downstairs. The scent of cinnamon had replaced the coffee, and she was delighted to see her mom's homemade cinnamon buns on the counter, cooling. Hayden was surprised that her mom was not in the kitchen, but there was a note on the table saying she was outside.

Hayden savored her soft, fresh cinnamon bun and a cup of tea. Heading out to the back porch, she put on an old jacket and slipped on some rubber boots. There were always a few extra pairs out there. The morning was damp, and everything smelled sweet and fresh. She wandered around the outside of the house, admiring all of her mom's perennial plants in bloom, almost identical to those of Lena's.

She found her mom over by the barn, leaving kibble out in plastic dishes for the barn cats.

"Good morning, you're up!" her mom greeted her.

"Yes, sorry I slept so long. I am post-night shift." Hayden yawned. "Your flower gardens look beautiful, Mom. Lena's are all in full bloom, too."

"Oh, how is Lena?" her mom asked.

"I am not sure. She seemed sad when I left. She did tell me to say hello to you all."

Hayden's mom took her on a tour of the vegetable garden that was out past the barn. It was twice the size of Lena's and a little more ahead in growth. Like Lena's, there was a wooden stake with the seed package overtop of it, designating the vegetable at the head of each row.

"Paddy really helped me with planting it this year." Winnie smiled. "He is also really helping your dad a lot, but I think your dad might either sell a lot of the cattle this spring or maybe get a hired hand for the summer."

"It's getting too much?" Hayden asked.

Winnie just nodded. Hayden decided not to press the issue.

It was too muddy to help her mom weed the garden or to drive out to the pasture. Just then, her dad and Paddy came around the corner on the gator with Butch perched in the back flatbed.

"Hey, Paddy, do you want to drive into town? I was going to pick up a bottle of wine for dinner, and we can stop by *Blainey's Bakery* for a cheese roll." Hayden offered, knowing the bakery run was a favorite ritual they enjoyed.

"Yes, please, Sister!" Paddy jumped out.

"You don't need to get wine for dinner, Hayden," her mom interjected. "And Paddy, you will need to change out of your muddy boots." Paddy was already running into the back porch.

"Anything you need in town, Mom?" Hayden offered.

"No, we're good, honey. I am doing a roast for dinner if that is okay."

"I'm up for that!" Ced clapped his work gloves together.

Hayden went in to get her purse. She decided to text Jean Marc back.

I'll be home tomorrow evening if you are free. We can just do coffee if you want. Hayden.

Hayden and Paddy drove into town. On the way in, they bantered about their favorite country songs. Paddy shared a love of country music with Hayden.

"I am eighteen this year, Hayden. Maybe I can have some wine with dinner tonight," Paddy announced as they neared the town limits.

"I'm not sure about that, Paddy. You will have to check with Mom and Dad about that." Hayden smiled and looked over at Paddy in the passenger seat.

They drove through town, and as they passed the *MacNamara Hotel and Tavern*, they saw the Royal Canadian Mounted Police (RCMP) patrol car parked outside. Hayden thought back to her first alcoholic drink at the 'Mac' bar. It had been a Singapore Sling.

That's my Sweetness, ordering a fruity drink on her eighteenth! Come on, be more adventurous!

"Someone is in big trouble!" Paddy blurted.

"Not necessarily, Paddy. Maybe they are just helping someone."

They drove down Main Street and made their purchase at the liquor store and then stopped in at *Blainey's Bakery*, angle parking in front. When they walked into the bakery, they both took a big, long inhalation. The aroma inside of a bakery was one of the best smells in the world. They chose their cheese rolls and headed back to the car.

"I think that's everything, Paddy. Let's head home for supper!" Hayden smiled, pulling back out onto Main Street.

"Do you need to pick up flowers, Hayden? Do we have to stop anywhere else?" Paddy solemnly asked.

Thank goodness the only light on Main Street had turned red at that moment. Hayden kept her eyes straight ahead as they filled with hot tears. She clutched the steering wheel tightly.

"Not today, Paddy," she said softly. The light turned green, and they headed back to the Barrett ranch in sad silence.

CHAPTER 7

Sweet Treats and Stampede

Hayden enjoyed the rest of her visit with her family and headed back to Calgary the next day after lunch.

Before she left, her dad hugged her and whispered in her ear, "Don't wait so long to come out next time, Bunny."

She arrived back in Calgary at around 2:30 p.m. Her mom had sent leftovers for her, and she unloaded everything from her vehicle. On her drive back to the city, Shelby had called her back on the Bluetooth and said that she and Dean were sick with a stomach bug, so a visit was not a good idea. Hayden promised to keep in better touch. One of the babies started to fuss, so the conversation was cut short.

Hayden texted Jean Marc, who texted her back quickly. He said he was working but would be off at 1800. Could they meet at Starbucks by the hospital?

No thanks to another first date at Starbucks, thought Hayden. She texted back an alternative.

How about meeting at Sweet Treats off Sunnyside Blvd? 1830?

He agreed to that. Now she needed to keep herself occupied for her nerves. She went upstairs and knocked on Lena's door.

Lena answered, and Hayden offered to take Finnegan for a walk along the river.

"Sure, dear, that would be great. He would love that. Let me get his leash." Lena went to get Finnegan and his leash. When she returned, Hayden noted she still had that air of sadness about her.

The wind was slightly cool, but the sun was still shining. Hayden and Finnegan had a good hour-long walk along Memorial Drive, which had a beautiful walking and bike path next to the Bow River. The river was high and moving quite swiftly, filled with the spring runoff from the nearby Rocky Mountains. It was the color of café au lait. There were pairs of Canada geese with their babies down along the riverbank, making the occasional honk.

Upon their return, Lena invited Hayden in for a cup of tea. *Perfect,* she thought. *I can ask some questions.* Any question was quickly answered when she entered the kitchen—the dining table was filled with pamphlets for seniors' assisted living complexes.

"What's all this about, Lena? Are you thinking of moving?" Hayden said in a concerned voice.

"Well," she hesitated, "I don't want to move, but Larry wants me to. He thinks I am a liability here. He said I would like it more at these facilities." Lena's eyes filled with tears.

Hayden was too shocked to say anything. *What was Larry's sudden motive for her to move?*

Hayden did her best to console Lena over tea. She seemed a bit more chipper after chatting with Hayden. A visit over tea was always an enjoyable time with Lena. She would often share stories of her happy memories of married life with Henry, and sometimes, Hayden would tell her snippets about her love life.

Hayden went back to her place at about 4:30 p.m. She had a long, luxurious bubble bath and then got ready. At just after six, she drove to *Sweet Treats*. Surprisingly, she wasn't feeling nervous.

Their date was wonderful. They talked mainly about Jean Marc and his upbringing in Montreal. His parents were divorced, and he had one sister, Esme, who still lived in Montreal. Hayden had never been to Montreal and only spoke a spattering of French from school. Jean Marc made the city sound so wonderful and metropolitan. Then Hayden confessed she was a bit nervous about going on a date with someone from work. Jean Marc laughed and smiled with those fabulous blue eyes.

Time flew by, and they both were surprised when the shop owner told them they were closing. Jean Marc walked her out to the parking lot next to her car. It was dark, and he pulled her close and kissed her.

"A bientot," he whispered in her ear. "See you soon."

Hayden drove home elated. That night, she slept soundly and could not remember her dreams in the morning. It was back to work.

Hayden worked the next three days on the day shift in the ICU. All were busy shifts, and she would see Jean Marc occasionally on the unit, although he was working in CCU for two of the shifts. There was prolonged eye contact and secret smiles between them, and he would come over and chat with her but always kept it on a professional level. They texted flirty texts in the evening when she would be home from work.

For two of her shifts, Hayden had the pleasure of working with Dr. Bernie Maplind as her resident. Bernie was so kind, and Hayden decided, quite brilliant. He was calm at the bedside with any deteriorating patient and so polite and approachable with all the staff. During doctors' rounds, he always had the right answer, and Hayden could see he was well respected by the intensivist. But then there was Louise.

Hayden had the misfortune of being on every coffee break at the same time as Louise. She frequently monopolized any conversation with *her* experience or *her* story. Their co-workers' faces, although doing their best to be polite, could not always hide their exasperation with Louise's antics. One lunch, it was how she decided that she and Bernie should convert to eating exclusive vegan. On a coffee break, it was how Bernie's parents LOVED her cooking when she had them for dinner. Another time was how she loved driving Bernie's Land Rover and hated going back to driving her crappy car.

On Hayden's last day shift, she entered the break room for her morning coffee break. Louise was in there alone.

"Hayden! I am glad we finally get to talk…alone," Louise began in a conspiring voice. "So, Bernie and I would love to get together with you and Jean Marc, go for dinner or something! This will be SUCH a fun summer for us!"

Hayden paused, not knowing what to say. "Um, well, Jean Marc and I are not a couple, Louise. We have only been on one date, and that is confidential."

"Oh, your secret is safe with me, sister!" Louise giggled. "I am confident that it will progress to something more for you both."

Just then, Alana walked into the break room. "Hey Hayden, I was just down in Emergency getting some suture material, and I saw Clairese. She says you are ignoring her!"

"Oh, my gosh. I know. I need to text her," Hayden agreed.

"Been a bit preoccupied?" Alana said with a sly smile.

Hayden looked at Louise, who lifted her eyebrows and smiled, then looked away.

"Anyway," Alana continued, "Clairese invited us all to the big annual ER/EMS/CPS Stampede event at the *Crossroads Beer Garden*. It is only a few days away! We gotta go; it is always a hoot!"

"I'm in!" laughed Hayden.

"Oh, us too!" exclaimed Louise.

The next few days flew by and were filled with walks with Finnegan, brief dinners with Jean Marc, and some steamy make-out sessions at Hayden's place. Jean Marc could never stay long as he had to get home to study, or he had an early shift the next day.

The day before the big Stampede event, Hayden received a call offering her an overtime shift for an eight-hour day. She accepted it, grateful for the extra money. Jean Marc had worked the night before, so she didn't see him on the unit. The shift was busy, and Hayden was happy to savor some summer day still when she headed out to the parking lot at 3:30 p.m. As she neared her car, she saw something white fluttering under the windshield wiper. Pulling it out, she read:

To the cowgirl that drives this horse! I can't wait to party it up with you tomorrow night! JM

Hayden's heart skipped a beat, and she smiled and got in her car. *She couldn't wait either*!

The next evening, Hayden took an Uber over to Jean Marc and Bernie's place at about 5:30 p.m. She was dressed western in jean shorts that showed off her legs, a white eyelet top that hugged her figure, cowboy boots, and a hat. She had braided her hair. She was feeling quite confident in her outfit.

Bernie's parents had purchased an upscale infill house for him in the community of Kensington, which was a very trendy neighborhood. From what she understood, Jean Marc paid Bernie some rent, but she wasn't sure how much. Hayden knew that Louise stayed there a lot but had not officially 'moved in.'

"Oh my God, you look so cute!" Louise exclaimed as Hayden walked in. Hayden wasn't quite sure by the look on her face if Louise was jealous or genuine. Louise was wearing a jean skirt and a tight yellow shirt, tied at the waist. Her breasts were spilling out the front. "You look great too!" Hayden replied, thinking, 'OMG.'

"This is a great place," Hayden said as she looked around. It did not look like two medical residents lived here. The furnishings were upscale with art on the walls, although it was all very masculine.

"I am trying to get them to buy some plants or something to make it homier!" Louise laughed. "It feels a bit like a show home or a museum to me."

Bernie and Jean Marc came up from the basement with beers in their hands. Bernie was in jeans and a western shirt and cowboy hat. He actually looked great. Jean Marc looked awkward. He, too, was wearing jeans, but he had a dress shirt on and no cowboy hat.

"What, no cowboy hat?" Hayden teased as she walked over to him. She leaned over to kiss him, which he reciprocated, but there was a hesitation on his part.

"I'm not really into this cowboy shit!" he scoffed.

Hayden was a bit nervous that this outing with their colleagues would make it 'official' that they were seeing each other. Maybe that was what Jean Marc was feeling too?

After having a drink, the four of them headed over to the *Beer Gardens* at the Crossroads Hotel. As they exited the Uber, Hayden reached for Jean Marc's hand, but he was already a step ahead of her. Louise clung to Bernie's arm.

They waited in line briefly, and when they entered, Jean Marc and Bernie immediately went over to the bar. Louise and Hayden made their way over to their group from the ICU. When they arrived, everyone was well ahead on the beverage consumption! There was a communal hoot when they walked up and lots of sloppy hugs.

"Does this mean you are besties now with Louise?" Ally slurred in her ear.

"I don't think you need to worry about that, Ally!" Hayden laughed.

Jean Marc and Bernie arrived with drinks, and the collective hoot was repeated. Jean Marc handed her a beer and squeezed her butt discreetly.

"Bottoms up, cowgirl!" he winked.

The night was a blast with everyone, but it was evident that there was not going to be any handholding or arms around each other with Jean Marc.

Halfway into the night, Hayden heard a loud familiar voice. "Coyote! There you are!" Clairese staggered over with her arm around a guy that looked significantly younger than her.

"So, what the hell, are you two a couple or what?" Clairese gestured to Jean Marc and Hayden with the beer in her hand. Clairese never minced her words, sober or drunk.

"Clairese!" Hayden hissed.

"I've been busy dancing all night here with Jayden…" Clairese squeezed her young cowboy.

"Jason," he corrected.

"Right! Anyway, I hadn't seen you and am so glad to see you now! Let's get together soon, Coyote!" and off Clairese went to the dance floor with Jayden/Jason.

"Who is that again?" Jean Marc asked disparagingly, "and why is she calling you Coyote?"

"It is my friend Clairese. She works in the ER. The Coyote name is a long story."

"Ah yes, I recognize her now from emergency. How old do you think her friend is?" he snorted.

Hayden never answered but instead replied, "Let's go get another drink."

Hayden had been disappointed to learn that Jean Marc did not know how to two-step or, for that fact, that he didn't like to dance. So, they spent the night visiting with everyone and drinking.

In the Uber drive back to Hayden's house, Jean Marc and Hayden sat in the back seat. Jean Marc chatted away with the Uber driver, at the same time with his hand discreetly down the front of Hayden's shorts. She was confident the driver could not see as she had her cowboy hat in her lap, but she was too drunk to care.

Back in her suite, they had quick, hot sex for the first time, and Jean Marc quickly passed out after that. Despite being very intoxicated, Hayden lay there with a sense of satisfaction but also with an inkling of something else, but she couldn't put her finger on it.

The next morning, Hayden woke up first with a massive headache. She got up and got some Tylenol and a drink of water. She climbed back into the bed, and Jean Marc rolled over.

"Good morning." he smiled. He reached and pulled her into his arms. Hayden lay there contentedly. "I think we need to get something straight."

Hayden pulled back to face him. "Okay?"

"I am not really a PDA kinda guy. I hope you won't be offended. I am just not into the 'holding hand, arms around each other' stuff. I promise you; I will make up for it here." With that, he squeezed her breasts and leaned over and kissed her deeply.

Hayden pulled back again to face him. "Is Bernie like that too? Louise seems to hang all over him."

"Why are you comparing me to Bernie?" Jean Marc frowned. "I am not comparing you to Louise."

"Believe me, I am not Louise!" laughed Hayden. She shared the 'Sealy Posturepedic' story with him. After she finished, she wondered if she had said too much. Would he be offended since Bernie was his friend? But Jean Marc laughed.

"Yeah, I think Louise is pretty insecure. However, I think she genuinely loves Bernie. I sometimes feel like she is my other roommate. Their sex life is a bit too vocal for me. So, I hope you don't mind if our 'intimate encounters' will always be here." He whispered the last line in her ear as he rubbed his hardness up against her.

Hayden lay back as he climbed above her. It was frenzied and passionate but very brief again. He rolled off her and stood up. It was the first time she saw him naked. She pulled the sheet over herself shyly.

"Can I shower here?" Jean Marc asked as he looked for his clothes.

"Of course!" Hayden paused, "Would you like some company? I can scrub your back."

"That is nice, but I gotta get back and study. I am back in ICU in two days."

Jean Marc showered while Hayden made some toast and tea. She pulled her hair in a ponytail and pulled on some leggings and a sweatshirt. He emerged from the bathroom in his clothes with wet hair. He looked so sexy. He smiled his charming smile, engaging her with his eyes.

"This was fun. Do you think you could drive me back to my place?"

"Oh, sure. I made some tea and toast if you want," offered Hayden.

"No, I'm good. I just really need to get back."

Hayden and Jean Marc headed upstairs and out to the garage. As they opened the door into the garage, Hayden was startled to find the garage door open and Larry and Jezz standing outside in the alley. It startled them as well, and they both looked at Jean Marc disapprovingly.

"Um, this is my friend, Jean Marc," she stammered. There was a collective nod between the men. Larry and Jezz did not explain what they were doing.

Hayden and Jean Marc got in her car and pulled out of the garage.

"They are charming," Jean Marc said sarcastically. "Why do I feel like I am the teenage boy caught by the dad in the girlfriend's bedroom?"

"I'm not sure," Hayden said nervously. "Yeah, they both creep me out."

They drove to Bernie and Jean Marc's. As they pulled up, Louise was outside on the front deck in a summer dress and sunglasses, drinking something orange. Bernie joined her on the deck just as Jean Marc opened the passenger car door.

"The only way to detox is to retox!" called Louise, toasting her glass in a cheers motion. She and Bernie both laughed.

"Come join us for mimosas!" they invited.

"Nah, I've got to study, gang!" Jean Marc shook his head.

He turned back and faced Hayden. "Like I said, this was really fun, especially, you know..." Jean Marc winked. "So, I will text you later. A bientot." He kissed her on the cheek and got out of her car.

Hayden smiled and then waved to Bernie and Louise. As she drove away, she was all warm inside, but she couldn't push away that feeling of uncertainty in the pit of her stomach.

I have to move on. It will be good with Jean Marc.

She took a deep breath to convince herself and then drove back home.

CHAPTER 8

A Hot July

The rest of July was an eventful one for Hayden. It was an unusually hot summer for southern Alberta, and that meant people were outside, frequently drinking, and often doing reckless things. This, more often than not, resulted in traumatic injuries, and so the ICU was busy with multi-system trauma patients for the month.

Hayden enjoyed sitting out in the backyard after her shifts. Lena had gone out to Kelowna, British Columbia, to visit her sister for ten days, so Hayden had agreed to look after Finnegan and water all her flowers every day. Hayden had driven her out to the airport, which she was more than happy to do, but questioned why Lena's own son hadn't stepped up to the responsibility. Larry had not been around lately, and she was thankful for that, especially if he had his creepy friend Jezz in tow.

She met Ally, Alana, and Shaye for lunch at an outdoor patio on their days off one day. She helped Clairese move some perennials in her yard, as she had recently bought an older little house by the hospital. "You know the most about plants, so I called on you! Please help me, Coyote!" she had begged her on the phone. They had a great time catching up, comparing, and exchanging ICU and ER work stories.

Clairese's love life was always a source of scandalizing entertainment too. She shared how her stampede friend, Jason/Jayden, had somehow gotten a hotel room that night, and they had had wild sex. He said he was stepping out to get drinks for them from the hotel vending machine in the hall and never returned. "But he left his fucking socks in the room!" Clairese screamed with laughter. Hayden didn't share that story with Jean Marc.

Jean Marc came over quite often, and Hayden cooked him dinner, which they would eat out on the back patio. Wine was a must. "French have wine with every dinner!" he would laugh. Hayden couldn't drink more than a glass and then be able to get up and function the next day. She wasn't sure how he did it and also be able to study. When they sat outside to eat, she would often secretly dump her wine in the grass.

One early August evening, they sat cuddled on the couch in her place. Jean Marc had his laptop open and was studying. Hayden was in a texting conversation with Shelby. She was making an effort to be in touch more often, and texting seemed to work best for Shelby, as she could answer when she was free. Shelby sent Hayden an adorable picture of the girls in matching pink outfits.

"Oh my gosh, look at this sweet picture of my friend Shelby's twin girls!" Hayden held her phone up for Jean Marc to see. He glanced over at the photo and responded, "cute," and looked back to his laptop.

"That's it?" she teased, "They are so adorable! And they are wearing the outfits I gave to her."

Jean Marc looked at her. "Yeah, kids are cute from a distance, and that's about it. I prefer adults, and that is why I will never work in pediatrics." He typed away on his laptop.

Hayden was quiet for a while, deep in thought. "So, does that mean you never want to have kids?"

"Not likely!" Jean Marc said distractedly, still typing.

"Hey, my sister Esme's birthday is at the end of August," he said cheerfully. "I will have a stretch of five days off right around then. Do you think you could get some time off, and we could fly to Montreal?"

Hayden was still stunned at his response to her question about kids. "Um, I'm not sure. We had to submit our request for vacation weeks back. Maybe I could trade some shifts with some people."

"You'll love Esme. She's very metropolitan. We can show you around Montreal. My mom might be there too with her boyfriend. Not keen to see that douche, but I definitely want to see my mom." He set his laptop down and pulled Hayden over in an embrace. "Hey, anything good to eat around here?" He nuzzled her ear.

"What did you have in mind? I have not gotten any groceries lately." she sighed.

"Well…if you are hungry. I'm delicious but not nutritious!" Jean Marc motioned to his crotch, indicating he wanted Hayden to give him oral sex.

Hayden rolled her eyes and got up. "I'll make us something."

"Oh, come on, girl!" Jean Marc flopped himself flat down on the couch. "I need an incentive to keep studying!"

"I probably should walk Finnegan again soon," she said as she opened the fridge, ignoring his comment.

Hayden made ham and cucumber sandwiches for lunch. As they sat down to eat, it was evident that Jean Marc was now grumpy.

"I think I am going to head home. I need some clean clothes, and I think Bern and I were going to quiz each other on an exam coming up."

Nothing more was said and Jean Marc brushed her cheek with a kiss and left to return home.

That evening, Hayden was speaking with her mom. She had confided weeks earlier that she and Jean Marc were seeing each other. Her mom was thrilled and encouraged Hayden to bring him down to the farm to meet the family. Tonight, she prodded Hayden again.

"When do we get to meet your fella, Hayden? I promise we will be on our best behavior, and Dad won't even call you Bunny!" she laughed.

"I am not sure if I am ready for that yet, Mom. But hopefully, I will bring him down sometime soon. I have some time off coming up next week, and I had planned to come down, just myself."

"Well, that would be great, Honey. You can come and help shell peas; we have a bountiful crop this year!" she replied brightly.

They finished their conversation, and then Hayden got ready for bed. Finnegan was curled up on her bed, next to her pillow. She climbed into the cool sheets and laid her head down with a heavy sigh. She was on duty the next morning, so needed a good night's sleep. Apparently, that was not to be. Hayden did not remember her dreams but woke up crying with Finnegan licking the tears on her cheeks.

CHAPTER 9

Travel Plans

The next day, Hayden worked in the CCU. Peggy officially announced that she was pregnant, and there was a consensus of congratulations and cheers. Hayden was so happy for her.

After Hayden had assessed her patients, Peggy came over to talk to her to get an update on the status of her assigned patients.

"I would really like to encourage you to apply for my clinician position while I am on maternity leave, Hayden. I think you would be great in the role," Peggy smiled. She was glowing. Pregnancy agreed with her.

"Well, thanks, Peggy. I appreciate it. I will take it under consideration. You look really happy by the way. Pregnancy looks great on you!"

"Thanks, Hayden! Someday, it will for you, too." Peggy smiled and walked away.

Hayden sat blankly at her desk. *Not likely!* Jean Marc's words echoed in her head.

Hayden kept busy on her shift with her three cardiac patients, who were all pleasant and hemodynamically stable. It was nice to have awake patients to converse with her while she assessed and cared for them.

At the end of her shift, she headed out to the parking lot. She was surprised to see Jean Marc's red Bronco parked in his usual spot. He was a creature of habit and parked in the same spot every shift, close to her usual spot since they had been seeing each other. As she approached her car, she saw a familiar white paper under her windshield wiper, fluttering in the wind. At first, her heart went in her throat when she reflected on their last interaction. He had not texted her all day. But then, she read the note.

Hey gorgeous, I had to pop in here for a meeting. Should be done by 1930. Come on over to ours; Bernie and Louise are cooking! JM xxoo

Hayden actually jumped with joy and then got in her car. She knew that Lena was home from Kelowna (she had called her on her lunch break). Larry had come through and had picked her up at the airport. Finnegan would not need to be walked or fed tonight.

Hayden headed over to Bernie and Jean Marc's. She contemplated going home to change out of her scrubs but then thought, forget it. She did stop and pick up a bottle of white wine, though.

"Hey, you're here!" Louise welcomed her at the door like it was her own house.

"I apologize for coming in my uniform."

"Not to worry! Come on in. Help yourself to the bunch of appetizers we have out and come grab a glass of vino."

Jean Marc arrived shortly after and came over and gave her a passionate kiss.

"Wowza!" Bernie exclaimed and laughed, looking over at them.

Hayden was shocked but pleased. Maybe his fear of PDA was waning.

The four of them sat out on the back deck, which was adorned with twinkling lights. They lounged in cozy cushioned patio furniture around a fancy fire 'bowl' with glass rocks, drinking wine and munching on delicious appetizers. It was a beautiful, warm summer evening in Calgary.

"Next time, you must bring your swimsuit, Hayden! Bernie's dad is installing a hot tub for us tomorrow. It will be just steps off this deck," Louise gushed.

"There will be rules around the hot tub, though," joked Bernie. "Swimsuits must be worn and there is to be no jiz in the tub!"

"Oh, gross!" Louise squealed and gave Bernie a shove on his arm.

Hayden laughed awkwardly and looked at Jean Marc, who she could see in the dim light, roll his eyes.

More wine, and then the conversation progressed to travelling.

"When we are done the next rotation, we will have a break in January for two weeks. I think we should all go on a trip!" proposed Bernie.

"That's an awesome idea, Bernie! The four of us would have a blast!" Louise agreed.

"Maybe for you, my man, who has an endless supply of money," Jean Marc lamented loudly.

"I have a friend who is a travel agent and could look for a deal for us." Hayden volunteered.

"There is still such thing as a travel agent? I thought everyone did everything online nowadays." queried Bernie.

"Well, she lives in the small town where I am from and works for Co-Op Travel."

"Yeah, Hayseed here from small-town Alberta can get us a deal!" Jean Marc toasted his glass in the air. "Well, you contact her and see what she can find for a group of four next January!"

Hayden could see that the effects of the wine were reaching Jean Marc.

"Didja look into doing the tradesy thing to go to Montreal with me at the end of August?" Jean Marc asked, now slurring his words.

"Well, I need to know the exact dates from you," she replied.

"I promise I will get them for ya," he winked at her and patted her leg clumsily.

The night ended shortly after, and amazingly, Jean Marc invited her to sleepover. But as soon as they lay on the bed, Jean Marc passed out.

The next morning, she awoke to his caress. She lay still as he stroked her body, enjoying this attention from him. She opened her eyes and smiled at him. He must have taken that as an invitation, as he immediately straddled her and began thrusting into her. Her passion began to mount, but then, she knew he was done. He lay on top of her, sweaty and panting.

"Great way to start the day off!" he kissed her quickly and then rolled off her. She closed her eyes, disappointed and unfulfilled.

"What are your plans for the day?" he asked as he grabbed a T-shirt to pull on.

"Not sure," she replied. "I am going home for a couple of days, come Friday."

"Hey, here are those dates at the end of the month. I would love for you to come to Montreal." He handed her a yellow sticky note that he had written the dates on.

"Well, speaking of which, I was wondering if you would like to come down to Willow Creek and meet my family sometime soon?" she said tentatively.

Jean Marc turned around with his eyebrows raised. "Well, are you sure your parents are ready to meet me?" He climbed back on the bed and crawled over to her.

"I think so," she smiled.

"Well, if you think they are ready to meet this charming doctor, then I think I am ready too, Hayseed!" he said affectionately and kissed her on the lips.

Hayden took a deep breath. *Was she really ready*?

CHAPTER 10

Chunk

Hayden worked two more shifts that week and then, as planned, drove home for two days. Jean Marc was going to be working in CCU for the weekend, so it worked out great because she would not have been able to see much of him.

Before she left, she texted Jean Marc the bad news:

I tried my best, but I can't trade those shifts for Montreal. I am so sorry! You'll still have fun with Esme. I hope you have good shifts! Love, Hayden xxoo

They had not said "I love you" to each other yet, and Hayden had hesitated if she should sign the text 'love.' They usually just put their initials and kisses and hugs. Hayden decided to take the plunge and sign it with 'love.'

Was she in love with him? She sat and contemplated it.

He texted her back quickly:

No worries, Hayseed! I understand. Have fun at the farm. Don't forget to see your travel agent friend. JM xxoo

She was disappointed he did not reciprocate with the salutation, but she decided not to dwell on it. She was actually more annoyed that he kept calling her 'Hayseed.' At first, it had been cute; now, it was just fucking annoying. She made a mental note that she was going to tell him to stop. *Open communication in any relationship is important, Hayden,* her mom had always told her.

But that honesty sometimes leads to tragedy, doesn't it, Hayden? She pushed that thought away.

She cranked her country tunes playlist and headed on the road. Jean Marc hated country music, so she only listened to it when she was alone.

It was a beautiful sunny day, and the road was wide open. She admired the patchwork of colored fields; there were still some late yellow canola fields in bloom. She sang along with the songs and enjoyed her drive. The approach for her town was ahead, and Hayden took the turn off onto the secondary highway and aimed her car towards Willow Creek. She could see the welcome sign for Willow Creek approaching in the distance. She took a deep breath and slowed the car. She looked in the rear-view mirror, and no one was behind her. As her car slowed, she pulled to the side of the road, the crunch of the gravel under her tires. She looked across the road at the wrought-iron gate. She stared at the inscription. 'At rest.'

What a stupid inscription her thoughts screamed! *Why not just say it like it is? Cemetery! Graveyard! Tomb! Mausoleum! Burial ground!*

She closed her eyes and took a deep breath. *I am not in the right frame of mind to go in.* Hayden checked her rear-view mirror and then pulled out, headed for town.

Once she got into town, she drove over to the Co-Op grocery store. It was the only grocery store in town, but other nearby towns were only, at the most, twenty minutes away if you wanted to shop somewhere else. There was also a little store in town called *Gordon's Grocery*. It had some basics: milk, bread, soft drinks, as well as odds and ends. It also had a little candy counter where you could buy mini paper bags of 'penny candy,' as her dad would call it.

She headed into the Co-Op grocery store and realized that she was starved. They had a deli counter that served sandwiches and, most recently, sushi! She opted for a hot chicken sandwich, as they were the best!

"Hi, Hayden," the girl behind the deli counter greeted. "I didn't know you were in town."

"Hi, Sheila," Hayden smiled. "I'm just in town for a couple of days seeing the family."

Sheila had gone to school with Hayden, and Hayden was not particularly fond of her. She was two-faced and the biggest gossip in town. However, Sheila was frequently the source of the gossip. Sheila and her now ex-husband had had run-ins with the RCMP for domestic violence and drugs.

Hayden ordered her sandwich and then sat at a nearby bench in the store to eat. Then she made her way over to the little side office in the store. Thankfully, Bronwyn was at her desk.

"Hayden Barrett! I didn't know you were in town!" Bronwyn greeted her warmly.

Well, the town gossip knows now, so everyone else will know soon, too. Hayden thought, thinking of her interaction with Sheila.

"Hi, Bronwyn, it's so great to see you!" Hayden said genuinely. Bronwyn was the younger sister of Liam Markas, who Hayden had gone to school with. Bronwyn was a sweet young woman and had a great reputation in her job for organizing wonderful vacations for Willow Creek residents.

"So, what can I help you with? Bronwyn offered.

"Well, I am looking for a great deal for a trip for four people in January."

"Oh, are you and the family wanting to get away? Who will look after Ced's cattle?" Bronwyn exclaimed.

"Ah, no, it is for three friends and me." Hayden hesitated and then blushed. "Two couples."

Bronwyn stared at her for a few seconds, then blurted, "Oh my gosh, Hayden, that is great! I am so happy for you." She looked sympathetically at her. "It's about time."

Hayden ignored her last comment and then outlined dates, possible destinations, and other details. Bronwyn promised she would look at all possibilities and get back to her as soon as she could.

Hayden left the Co-Op and walked down the street to her favorite shop, *The Crow and Crocus*. It was a combination gift shop, floral arranger, and craft store. They always had unique little gifts and beautiful flowers and plants. She browsed and then chose a purple African violet for her mom. Hayden knew the sisters that owned the store, but the clerk ringing in her purchase said they were both busy making bouquets for a local wedding tomorrow.

Main Street was relatively quiet for midday on a Friday. Hayden walked back up towards her car parked at Co-Op. As she passed the MacNamara Hotel, the tavern door opened, and out stepped a familiar face.

"Chunk," Hayden said, her face drained of color. She stood awkwardly, holding her plant.

"Hi, Hayden," he replied. Although he was not swaying or slurring his words, she knew he was drunk. She could smell it on him as well.

They both stood on the sidewalk, lost in embarrassment, as they both searched for something to say.

"No one calls me that anymore, you know." Chunk chewed his lip and shoved back his dark brown hair off his forehead.

"Oh, I'm sorry…old habits….." Hayden stammered, realizing her choice of words was not appropriate.

Chunk looked at her African violet plant. "Is that for him?" he asked.

Hayden looked down at her plant. "Oh, ah no, no. This is for my mom. A gift."

"Have you been out there, I mean to the grave?" Chunk asked, looking away.

"No. I feel bad, but it is just too hard. I almost did on the way in today, but I couldn't do it," she replied softly. "How about you, Chunk?"

He contemplated this for a moment. "I go out when I know there is no one else around. I don't need judgy eyes looking at me. It is bad enough, just here around town." This time, he slurred his words a bit.

"Chunk…" Hayden began, then stopped. She was sure he had heard it all before.

They stood in silence again.

"You know, they said I am probably responsible for his death. I wasn't wearing a seatbelt, so my big drunk body here, tossed around in the truck and probably hit him. Broke his neck or something worse."

"Chunk!" Hayden put up her hand to make him stop.

"I'm sorry," he said softly. "It should have been me that died."

Hayden took a deep breath. She decided to change the subject. "Are you working?"

"Not when I am a fucking drunk!" He laughed sarcastically. "But don't worry, I don't drive. I just stagger home. I am living in a dumpy apartment across from the bank."

"I wish I could help you," Hayden said sincerely.

"I am sure you've got your own demons to deal with." Chunk looked her directly in the eyes. Hayden looked away.

"I do," she replied softly.

"How is Calgary?" he asked after a moment. "You still nursing at the hospital?"

"Of course, yes, it is going well." She tried to smile.

The awkward silence ensued.

"Well, I should go, Chunk. I mean Dylan. Take care of yourself."

Chunk hesitated like he was going to say something else. He just nodded and then walked in the direction of his apartment.

Hayden stood on the corner, staring down at her plant.

If she could only go back in time to that night with Wyatt and change everything.

CHAPTER 11

Wyatt

When Hayden started high school in Willow Creek, it gave her the opportunity to meet a whole new group of kids. Willow Creek Community High was the feeder school. It served many surrounding communities that only had schools that went as high as Grade 9.

Hayden was excited to attend high school and became involved in as much as she could. She sat on the student council, she sang in the school choir, and she was on the varsity track and the basketball team. In Grade 9, she had sprouted up past many of the boys and was nicknamed 'Spider' because her legs were long like a daddy longlegs. Initially, she was angry at the nickname, but she soon realized her long legs were to her advantage in sports.

Also making the basketball team was a girl named Shelby Montgomery. She lived on a farm forty-five minutes away from Willow Creek and had attended a different rural elementary and junior high. Ironically, their paths had never crossed, but their parents knew of each other. The two became fast friends and did everything together.

The summer of Grade 11, Shelby informed Hayden that her brother Wyatt was returning home. He was three years older than her and had been on the rodeo circuit as a saddle bronc rider but had become injured. After some heart-to-heart talks with his parents, he reluctantly decided to return home and help with his parent's expansive grain farm.

Hayden had just earned her driver's license, even though she had been driving on the farm for the past two years in the fields and on the gravel road for short distances. She begged her parents to let her drive to Shelby's farm for a sleepover, even though it was an hour away. After discussion between Ced and Winnie, they agreed, but she had to call as soon as she arrived.

When she pulled into the Montgomery farm, the first thing she saw was Wyatt Montgomery emerging from the barn, shirtless and sweaty. Tall and muscular and tan, he was quite the sight. He pulled his ball cap off a mop of black curly hair and wiped his brown, squinting into the sun as she got out of her vehicle.

"Hi, you must be Wyatt. I am a friend of Shelby's," she called and smiled her biggest smile.

"You have a name?" he smirked and then put his hands on his hips.

"I'm Hayden."

Just then, Shelby came running out of the house. "You made it! I'm so glad you are here!" she squealed.

Hayden grabbed her bag out of her car and proceeded to call her parents. As they neared the house, she looked back to see Wyatt leaning on a rake and staring at her. She smiled and went inside.

"You never told me your brother was so handsome, Shelby!"

"Yuck, Wyatt? Trust me, you don't want a rodeo boy like him!" warned Shelby.

"I thought you told me he quit?" Hayden asked as she put her things in Shelby's room.

"He did, but you still don't want him!" Shelby giggled.

The girls went for a ride on Shelby's horses. Wyatt helped the girls saddle them up. He was polite and sweet, and Hayden could not stop looking at him.

That night after dinner, Shelby had a call from Dean Winchester, a boy in their class. He was having a bush party out on his ranch and wanted to invite Shelby and encouraged her to bring any friends. The girls were excited, although secretly, Hayden just wanted to stay in and flirt with Wyatt.

Shelby was begging her parents, Tate and June, to let them go.

"I am not sure if Hayden's parents would allow her to go, especially if there is drinking there," June advised the girls.

"Well, my parents would allow anything that you would allow." Hayden smiled innocently, perhaps telling a bit of a white lie. She knew deep down that they would disapprove.

June and Tate exchanged glances. "Well, how about this," proposed Tate. "Wyatt, you can take the girls and drive them and supervise that they are not drinking."

"Come on, Dad," protested Wyatt. "I don't want to be a chaperone for a bunch of teenagers all night."

Wyatt and Hayden made eye contact. She smiled shyly and looked away. Surprisingly, Shelby did not put up a fight that her older brother would potentially be chaperoning. Hayden knew that Shelby just wanted to see Dean.

"Why not call up Chunk and see if he wants to join you? Then at least you will have someone your own age to talk to," suggested June.

Wyatt, June, and Tate agreed on the plan. The girls quickly grabbed their jackets and as they walked out the door, Tate yelled: "Remember what I said, no drinking!"

The trio jumped into Wyatt's truck. Hayden sat next to Wyatt. She was on cloud nine.

The bush party was such a great time. Wyatt's best friend Chunk arrived in his own truck. He was a huge dude: six foot three and probably 230 pounds. He had been offered a football scholarship for university but declined it to take plumbing at SAIT in Calgary and then work for his dad's business. He was hilarious and kept a group of them in stitches all night with his imitations and jokes.

Dean and Shelby were cuddled up, sitting on a log by the fire pit, drinking beers. They intermittently came and stood with Hayden, Wyatt, and Chunk's group.

Shelby whispered in Hayden's ear, "Are you okay? Do you mind that I hang with Dean?"

Hayden turned to Shelby, "It's no problem at all!" and grinned from ear to ear. In the dark, Shelby couldn't see that Hayden and Wyatt were holding hands.

By 2:00 a.m, Wyatt told Shelby they needed to leave. Chunk had already left in his truck, and Hayden was surprised, as she had seen him drink at least three beers. True to his word to his dad, Wyatt had not drunk a drop.

Shelby begged for five more minutes to go back to say goodnight to Dean. Hayden and Wyatt walked over to his truck. Hayden leaned up against the driver's door.

"Thanks for bringing us. This was super fun!" Hayden smiled.

"It was my pleasure. Thanks for coming out to the farm this weekend." Wyatt said lightly and chuckled.

Hayden was looking into his brown eyes, reflecting off the moon. She felt like she was melting.

"I am so glad I came back to Alberta," he said huskily and then leaned over and kissed her. It was long, sweet, and Hayden didn't want it to end.

From that moment, they were a couple, as were Shelby and Dean. Wyatt came over to her farm every weekend and even helped her dad on occasion. He played catch with Paddy in the yard, or the three of them would go for rides out in the field in the gator to check on cattle.

Ced, Winnie, and Paddy all loved Wyatt, and so did Hayden.

One Friday morning that first summer, Wyatt pulled into her yard in his truck. Ced, Winnie, and Paddy were getting ready to drive into the city for a doctor's appointment for Paddy. They were planning to stay overnight.

"We will be back tomorrow afternoon, Hayden. Are you staying here with Shelby, or are you going to stay at her place?" her mom asked.

"The plan is, she is coming here, Mom," Hayden said.

"Okay, just checking. Make sure you feed Butch tonight. Be good," Winnie said, lifting one eyebrow at Hayden. It was unspoken words: *Wyatt is not to stay here.*

"Are you up for an adventure, Sweetness? Wyatt asked, kissing her after her family had driven away.

"Sure!" Hayden replied enthusiastically. She locked the house, and minutes later, they were en route into Willow Creek.

"What are we doing?" she asked curiously, then looked in the back of the truck.

"No peeking! It is a surprise!"

They passed the town limits, and Wyatt turned down a dirt path in his truck. It wound down a small hill to a treed area near the creek. It was very secluded.

"How'd you know about this place?" Hayden teased. "Have you brought lots of girls down here before?"

"Only you." he smiled. "Years back, the boys and I used to come down here to drink. I have not been down here in a couple of years."

Wyatt then pulled out a blanket, a picnic lunch, and a bottle of wine.

"I can't take credit for the food; my mom made it. But I snuck the bottle of wine." Then he pulled out a rose and handed it to her.

Hayden was floored. They ate the lunch, felt giddy with the wine, and then made love for the first time on the blanket under the sun. Wyatt was patient and gentle and had obviously been anticipating this as he came prepared with a condom.

They spent the whole afternoon there. As they lay naked on the blanket, under the warm summer sun, neither of them was modest or shy. They took each other in. Wyatt teased her about her long legs.

"Long legs like these are a jockey's dream!" he teased as he caressed her legs.

"Are you calling me a horse?" she teased back and rolled on top of him.

"Not at all, Sweetness." he smiled and then kissed her deeply.

Hayden's rose was wilted by the end of the hot afternoon in the sun. "Throw it in the creek and make a wish!" he encouraged.

She made her wish: *I wish that I will always be happy with Wyatt* and threw the rose into the water. She watched it float down the creek until she couldn't see it anymore.

That night, Shelby *did* sleepover at Hayden's house, but so did Dean and Wyatt. Wyatt and Hayden spent most of the night lovemaking until they fell asleep in each other's arms at 4:00 a.m.

The rest of the summer was spent at parties together with Dean and Shelby, and Chunk too. There were so many laughs and good times. Hayden suspected her parents knew that she and Wyatt were intimate, but she still had to be discrete. There were interludes in the hayloft in the barn, the back of his truck, and, of course, in their houses if their parents weren't home.

Autumn came, and her final year of high school was ahead. The year was busy with her studies, basketball, applying for scholarships, and deciding what university she wanted to apply to. She was set on nursing as her career choice. She sent her application to three universities, all in Alberta. She hoped she would be accepted to Lethbridge so that she could be close to home, but most of all, close to Wyatt.

One Saturday, Shelby, Hayden, and their moms drove into Calgary to pick out their graduation dresses. It felt like they were choosing wedding dresses.

"That may not be too far off for me, Hayden." Shelby confided to her one night on the phone. "Dean and I want to get married soon. Dean will go to Olds College for his agriculture mechanic certificate, and we just don't want to be apart. I hopefully can get a job there in town while he is at school." Hayden was shocked.

Wyatt was at every basketball game, usually with Chunk and Dean, cheering Shelby and Hayden on. When her birthday came in the spring, she was the last to turn eighteen.

"It is tradition in Willow Creek to go to the *Mac* for your first legal drink!" Chunk had laughed with the group. "Let's take her there." There were twelve of them at the table, and Hayden decided on a Singapore Sling as her drink of choice.

"What, no shot of tequila?" Chunk cackled.

"That's my Sweetness, ordering a fruity drink on her eighteenth," Wyatt smiled adoringly at her. "Come on, be more adventurous, have a beer!" he teased.

Hayden stuck to her choice, regretting it later. What had Chunk said? *Beer before liquor, never been sicker; liquor before beer, you're in the clear.* It didn't work for her, regardless.

One spring evening, Wyatt and Hayden drove out to their secret spot. Hayden was terrified the truck would get stuck in the mud. They lay under blankets in the bed of the truck, with only the moonlight lighting their faces.

"I've been accepted to the Lethbridge College for nursing, Wyatt," Hayden said quietly.

Wyatt sat up. "That is great, Hayden! I am so proud of you."

Hayden looked up at his face in the moonlight. He had never been more handsome. She loved him so much, but she was worried about being apart so much for the next four years. She shared her anxiety with him.

"I will wait for you, Hayden. I know that you are the one that I want to spend my days and nights with. And you are only like, an hour away. We can do the long-distance thing." He looked down at her and smiled reassuringly.

"Are you sure? I know you have dated other girls, and I don't want to hold you back," Hayden said softly.

She saw him flinch, and then he was quiet. He turned and looked up at the moon. "Or is it that *you* want to meet other people?" he asked.

Hayden was quiet and then replied, "The thing is, I don't have anything to compare to. I really love you, Wyatt, but I want to be one hundred percent sure."

Wyatt turned back and gave her a sly smile. "Well, Sweetness, when you have perfection like us, you don't need to compare." He leaned over and kissed her.

June came, and graduation was a wonderful celebration. Shelby and Dean announced their engagement soon after, and no one seemed surprised. They set the date for their wedding that August and, of course, every gossip in town thought Shelby was pregnant. Truthfully, as she said, they just wanted to be together.

The wedding was in the Montgomery's backyard with just close family and friends. Hayden was the maid of honor, Wyatt and Chunk were groomsmen, and Paddy was a ring bearer. The reception and dance included many more friends and was at the Willow Creek Hall. What a party that was! They had a live band and danced the night away.

At 3:00 a.m, Wyatt was driving Hayden back to her farm. Winnie and Ced had offered to let Wyatt sleep on the couch, as they knew it would be a late night.

As they drove down the gravel road, they sang along to a favorite country song.

"Oh, I wished they would have played this tonight to dance to. I love this song!" Hayden sighed.

Suddenly, Wyatt pulled off to the side of the road and drove into a turnout in a cornfield.

"Wyatt, what are you doing? We should not be going into this person's field!"

"This is Doug Kendrick's field, and he is a cocksucker, so he can lose a few stalks of corn!" Wyatt laughed.

Wyatt jumped out of his side of the truck and put his hand out. "Out you get, Sweetness," he instructed. He restarted the song and cranked the volume.

There, at 3:00 a.m at the edge of a cornfield, they danced in the bed of his truck— bridesmaid dress, tux, and all.

"I will never forget this!" Hayden smiled up at him in the moonlight.

"Neither will I," he said and pulled her close.

CHAPTER 12

Ladybugs

After her encounter in town with Chunk, Hayden drove home to the farm for the weekend. She didn't tell her parents about what happened but instead chattered with her mom about work, Peggy's pregnancy, and her encouragement to apply for the clinician position. As usual, her mom filled her in on what was the latest news in town. Hayden wondered if anyone had seen her conversation on the street with Chunk.

The next day, she sat on the porch and shelled peas with her mom, weeded in the garden, checked cows with her dad and Paddy, and walked the gravel road with Butch for exercise. She planned to visit Shelby and Dean, and the girls tomorrow on her drive back to the city.

The next morning, she and Paddy went out and threw the ball in the yard. Paddy lost interest in it after ten minutes, so they sat down in the grass near a weeping willow tree.

"Let's look for four-leaf clovers, Sister!" Paddy laughed.

Hayden found a piece of quackgrass, put it between her thumbs, and tried to make it whistle with no success.

"Hayden, look what I found!" Paddy called her excitedly.

She looked over to see a ladybug crawling on his hand. "Oh! Be very careful with her, Paddy." She didn't want him to squish it.

"Sing the song, Hayden!" Paddy insisted.

"Ladybug, ladybug, fly away home, your house is on fire, and your children are alone!" Hayden began. *What a horrible rhyme*, she thought.

Paddy laughed.

Hayden closed her eyes. She thought back to the last time she saw a ladybug up close.

The summer after her first year of college, Hayden and Wyatt were down at their secret creek spot. They were lying on the blanket after a lovemaking session and a skinny dip in the creek. Wyatt was dozing in the warm sun, and Hayden was lying on her side, contentedly watching him. Suddenly, she saw a ladybug crawl on his shoulder. She woke Wyatt and showed him.

"You know ladybugs are good luck?" He smiled at her and traced a finger down her cheek.

"Okay, I will remember that. So, does that mean good luck for you because she was crawling on your shoulder or good luck for me since I was the one that saw her?"

"I guess it is good luck for both of us, Sweetness."

Hayden's memory was interrupted by Winnie, calling in Paddy and Hayden for lunch from the front porch. Paddy ran over to Winnie to show her his bug.

After lunch, Hayden packed up her things and headed out on her drive to Shelby and Dean's. They lived in Willow Creek in a cute little three-bedroom house on the edge of town. Winnie sent a casserole, homemade jam, and pickles for them.

Her visit with Shelby and Dean was wonderful. She was nervous arriving, concerned that they would be disappointed in her lack of communication. If they were upset, there was no indication of it in their visit. They were so wrapped up in caring for their twins.

Both were very hands-on parents, and despite the lack of sleep, they looked so happy with their family.

Hayden contemplated telling them about her encounter with Chunk but decided against it. They never brought him up, and she was confident that they were well aware of his state, especially since they lived in town.

Wyatt's name was not brought up, either. His picture was prominently displayed with a grouping of some family photos. She knew if Shelby had given birth to boys, that one would have been named Wyatt.

However, Shelby *did* ask if she was seeing anyone.

"Well," she stammered, "yeah, I have been seeing this resident, but it is nothing serious." She lied, and she instantly felt guilty. *You are bringing him home to meet your family in two weeks! Shelby is your best friend.*

There was an awkward silence, and then they both said in unison to Hayden, "Well, that is great!"

Hayden said she needed to get back on the road. They each hugged her, and Hayden kissed the girls on their heads as they slept. Before she left town, she checked her phone to see a text from Bronwyn.

Found a great deal for you and your friends! Give me a call! B

CHAPTER 13

Living on the Edge

Hayden elected to head back to Calgary before calling Bronwyn. She had to work the day shift tomorrow and still had some errands to run for the rest of the day.

Calgary's weather was cool, windy, and overcast. When she pulled into the garage, her stomach dropped as she saw Larry's Subaru parked inside. She gathered her belongings and headed into the backyard. Larry and Jezz were in the yard wearing matching windbreakers and were discussing something as she entered the yard. She looked down to see Jezz had a measuring tape in his hand. When he saw her looking at it, he instinctively put his hand behind his back. His face alternated between looking hostile and just flat. Larry appeared straight-up guilty.

"Hello," Hayden said flatly. "What are you up to?" She looked around to see any sign of Lena but didn't even see her looking out the window.

"Well, *we* are thinking of helping Mom by extending this patio here," Larry replied in a fakely sweet voice, emphasizing the 'we.' "This garden is just getting too much for her, and we worry about her."

Hayden was stunned at first but then spoke up. "Larry, you know this garden is her pride and joy, and she has never indicated that it was too much for her. I can help…"

Jezz cut her off. "I think you should mind your own business, Missy. After all, you are just the renter!" He turned his head slightly and smiled contemptuously.

"Jezz..." Larry began, putting his hand up, indicating for him to stop.

Hayden didn't know what else to say, so just brushed past them. "Excuse me."

She went in the back door, but as she reached back to close the screen, she looked back at them. Larry was leaning down, measuring something, and Jezz was staring back at Hayden with a thin smile of satisfaction on his face.

Hayden felt so upset by this encounter that she felt nauseous. She decided to skip some of her errands, at least until they left the yard. She also vowed that she would go and talk to Lena when they weren't around.

Grabbing her phone to call Bronwyn back, it buzzed in her hand.

Are you back yet? I hope you had fun and caught up with your family and country bumpkin friends! JM xoxo

She was annoyed with the 'country bumpkin' reference. She thought back to her last forty-eight hours back at home. She had not told Jean Marc about Wyatt yet. He hadn't really asked her about her past relationships.

Hayden elected to call Bronwyn back first. She outlined a couple of options, all of which sounded exciting. Hayden promised to get back to her after speaking to the group. Bronwyn stated that she would need a deposit in the next week to hold the spots.

She made herself a cup of tea and sat back on her couch. She was starting to calm down after the encounter outside. Dialing Jean Marc's number next, he answered on the first ring.

"Bonjour, ma cherie!" he answered. Hayden smiled, but she was taken aback by his affectionate greeting, unusual for him.

"Are you home? Is this a good time to talk?" Normally, Hayden would text him first to make sure she wasn't interrupting him at work.

"I am just laying here, kinda studying but also dreaming of your luscious body." This time, Jean Marc slurred his words.

"Are you drinking? It is 4:30 in the afternoon!" Hayden said, laughing but also concerned.

"I just had some wine. It was a busy couple of shifts, and it helps wind me down."

Hayden decided not to dwell on it but instead outlined what Bronwyn had offered. Jean Marc loved the idea of Cancun. He said he would text Bernie and Louise and see what their thoughts were.

"Why don't you come over and we can order a pizza? I missed you," Jean Marc sighed.

"Okay," Hayden agreed. "But it won't be late as I have to work days tomorrow."

After getting off the phone, her stomach flip-flopped. Was this trip the right thing? She was confident she could get the time off since it was not until January. She wondered how she could get along with Louise for two weeks.

Hayden looked out her back window and saw that Larry and Jezz were gone. She slipped upstairs and knocked on the back door. She could hear Finnegan barking, but no one answered. Lena sometimes took afternoon naps and removed her hearing aid, so she might not hear Hayden knocking.

Hayden returned downstairs to grab her things before heading over to Jean Marc's. He had texted her.

Bern and Louise are in for Cancun! Let's book it, Seniorita! Can't wait!

See you soon, love JM xxoo

She raised her eyebrows at the salutation. She smiled and dialed Bronwyn's number, advising her of the dates and requesting to book it for the four of them.

"I will need a $1000.00 deposit for the four of you, Hayden, to hold this package," Bronwyn advised kindly.

Hayden hesitated but felt confident and gave Bronwyn her credit card number.

Hanging up, she felt excited and drove over to Jean Marc's. He answered the door shirtless and in sweatpants. He pulled her over to him and kissed her deeply.

"I missed you," he whispered sloppily in her ear.

Hayden giggled. "I think we need to get some pizza into you to dilute the wine, doctor."

Hayden ordered the pizza on his laptop while Jean Marc started caressing her. The minute she put down the computer, Jean Marc pulled off her shirt, followed by the rest of her clothes.

"Right here in the living room?" Hayden laughed. "What if Bernie and Louise come home?"

"They are gone for the weekend." He panted in her ear.

Seconds later, he was penetrating her, and before she knew it, he moaned, thrust, and collapsed. The whole encounter lasted less than three minutes.

"God, I missed you," he said into the pillow. He kissed her cheek.

Hayden lay on the couch, unfulfilled and disappointed again. Jean Marc got up, pulled up his sweats, and padded into the kitchen. "Want a glass of wine?"

"No, I am good," she declined, pulling on her clothes.

"How was your visit with your family?" He appeared with a new glass of wine but nothing to drink for Hayden.

"It was great. They are looking forward to meeting you in a couple of weeks."

"Me too." He smiled and kissed her again. "How old is your brother again?"

"He is eighteen," Hayden said. She opened her mouth to say more but changed her mind.

They cuddled on the couch and watched a show on TV. The pizza arrived. Hayden hadn't realized how famished she was until she started eating.

Jean Marc finished off the bottle of wine, and Hayden cleaned up the pizza box and plates.

"I should go since I am working day shift in the morning. Are you at the hospital at all tomorrow?" She asked into his hair as she hugged him goodbye.

"Yes," he groaned. "I am in for rounds in the morning and a seminar on intubation in the afternoon. I will pop by and see you maybe?" he offered.

"Sounds good." She pulled back and smiled as she grabbed her keys and stepped outside.

He stepped outside, almost stumbling, and then pulled her over to embrace her again. "I am really looking forward to this trip." He nuzzled her hair. "I love you, Hayden."

With that, he stepped back in, smiled, and shut the door.

Hayden drove home elated.

The next morning came too soon. She wanted to stay in her bed as she could hear the rain pelting the windows. Reluctantly, she climbed out of bed and got ready for work.

As she approached the female staff locker room, she could hear squeals and lots of people talking. She looked up to see Ally coming from the opposite direction, approaching the locker door as well.

"What is going on in there?" Ally laughed as she pushed open the door for them both.

Ally and Hayden stood at the door, looking at their group of colleagues crowded around Louise.

Louise's eyes lit up when she saw Hayden. "Hayden! I wanted you to be the first to know when we got home last night, but you had already left!" she exclaimed breathlessly. "Bernie and I got engaged last night!" Louise waved her left hand to show off her ring.

There was a collective squeal in the room. Louise waved her hand out for Hayden to see her ring. Hayden and Ally stepped over to admire it. It was at least a carat and a princess square cut, surrounded by tiny diamonds. It was stunning.

Ally and Hayden both genuinely congratulated her. This was followed by a flurry of questions from others: what is the date, where are they getting married?

Hayden and Ally stepped back out into the hall after putting their belongings in their lockers.

"Oh my God!" Ally groaned. "That is all we are going to hear about for the next six months! Every fucking minute detail of the wedding plans."

"Stunning ring, though." Hayden sighed. *So that is why they were away for the weekend.*

Hayden sat down in the break room next to Jonas, a male nurse from their team. Jonas was from the Philippines and had worked on the unit for about a year but was recently returning from a back injury.

"Where is everyone?" he asked, gesturing to the empty break room except for Ally, Hayden, and himself.

"Louise got engaged, and everyone is fawning over her ring in the locker room," Ally said flatly.

Jonas laughed. "Okay, makes sense."

"Good to have you back, Jonas," Hayden said genuinely. She liked Jonas, and he was a hard worker.

"Good to be back!" he grinned.

The locker room group spilled in, followed by Danni, looking as sullen as ever. She had divided her coarse, long red hair into two braids. She plunked her short, plump self down on the sofa and stared straight ahead.

Louise sat down across from Hayden; her face flushed. She placed each hand on a knee and kept looking down at her ring, rotating her left ring finger, watching the gems sparkle. She looked over at Hayden and caught her staring. Louise smiled.

Was that a bit of a smug smile? Hayden thought, but she reciprocated the smile.

Shaye was ill tonight, and Alana was off on vacation. As usual, Betty came flying in at the last minute, hair astray, looking like a tornado, just as Peggy and Carl were reading out the assignments for the ICU and CCU.

"I see some things never change," whispered Jonas to Hayden. They both smiled.

But Hayden had no idea how drastically things were going to change.

CHAPTER 14

The Trip Home

Ally had been right. For the next three day shifts, Louise brought in a pile of wedding magazines and on break, or at her bedside on downtime, spoke non-stop about what *she and Bernie* wanted for their big day.

"I doubt that Bernie has a fucking say in anything," Ally lamented to Hayden as they mixed medications for their patients in the med room. "Has Louise asked you to be in the wedding party yet?"

"No, she hasn't," Hayden replied. *She hasn't said much to me directly at all*, Hayden thought.

Ironically, Bernie was the resident on in ICU for today's day shift. Jean Marc was on in CCU. Bernie popped by Hayden's bedside as she changed her unconscious and ventilated patient's chest tube dressing.

"All good in here, Hayden?" Bernie smiled.

"Oh, hi, Bernie! All is good here. Congratulations, by the way! That is awesome for you and Louise."

"Yeah, we're pretty excited. We have not finalized a date, but I want you to know that the trip is still on for us. It will be fun with you and Jean Marc."

This relieved Hayden, as neither Jean Marc nor Louise had really addressed it since the big announcement. Jean Marc had sent her a text Monday afternoon after his seminar:

So, what do you think of the big news?

They had chatted on the phone last night and talked about it. Jean Marc shared that Bernie assured him that he could stay living at the house until their residency was over, and Jean Marc was grateful for that.

Hayden and Jean Marc were surprisingly able to grab lunch together on Tuesday in the cafeteria. He suggested that the four of them go for dinner to celebrate the engagement on Wednesday after their shift. Hayden thought it was a great idea.

On Wednesday, Hayden changed out of her scrubs at home and then swung by Jean Marc's so they could take one vehicle to the restaurant. They met at an Italian bistro not far from the hospital.

It was a pleasant evening, and they talked about the trip for January. Hayden mentioned that she had put the $1000.00 deposit down, and they all said they would square up the deposit between them 'soon.' *How difficult is an e-transfer?* she thought.

Hayden was the designated driver. As they got up from the table, she was grateful for that. She looked and realized that between the three of them, they had polished off three bottles of wine.

Louise had talked about the wedding at dinner, but there was no mention of her being part of the wedding party. Jean

Marc had told her last night that Bernie asked him to be his best man, even though he has two brothers.

As they headed into the house, Louise and Bernie went upstairs, saying goodnight to them both.

"Are you going to come in for a little French lovemaking?" Jean Marc whispered sloppily in her ear as he squeezed her breasts. Hayden looked over his shoulder at the couch where their last encounter was.

She pulled back to face him and lied. "My stomach is a bit upset after all that rich food. I am going to take a rain check, sorry." She leaned over and quickly kissed him on the lips. He held her face and kissed her back and pulled her in close again, pressing his hardness up against her. "Are you sure I can't change your mind?"

Hayden sighed. *Open communication is the key to a happy relationship.* Her mom's words rang in her ears. *Not tonight when he is drunk.*

"No, I don't think that is best. I'll call you tomorrow."

Hayden was crawling into her bed thirty minutes later when her phone buzzed. She looked and saw it was Jean Marc.

"Hey, what's up?" she asked.

"I'll tell you what's up," he whispered and laughed into the phone.

"Jean Marc, really?" she knew he was more drunk. "Why are you calling?"

"Don't be mad. I just phoned to tell you that I love you, Hayden."

Why can't you tell me that when you are sober?

"Jean Marc, why are you drinking so much these days? It is going to catch up with you and your studies," Hayden said in a concerned voice.

"I didn't call you to have you lecture me," he snapped.

"I am not lecturing you. I am just concerned, that's all."

"Okay," he said coldly. "I will talk to you later." And the phone clicked off.

Hayden slept a sleepless night. In the morning, she saw Lena out in the yard, watering her plants.

"Lena, I have been trying to visit you," Hayden greeted. "I have knocked on your door a couple of times."

"Oh, hello, dear," she said, turning off her hose. "I have been a bit under the weather."

"I am sorry to hear that, Lena. Is there anything that I can do to help?" she offered.

"No, Hayden," she smiled sadly.

Hayden hesitated. "I understand that Larry and his friend are wanting to change your patio back here."

"Yes, but I said no. This is my house, and I am not going to be bullied into doing something I don't want," Lena said firmly.

Hayden was relieved to hear Lena's stance on this. She smiled reassuringly at her. "Well, I am glad to hear that, Lena. Remember, I am always here to help. As a matter of fact, I am off today and would love to take Finnegan for a walk. Would that be okay?"

"Absolutely." Lena's face brightened. "Listen, I have some fresh banana muffins that I made for Mrs. Adams across the street. She has been struggling with her arthritis and high blood pressure lately. I made so many, and I would like for you to have some too."

Hayden went inside the kitchen to get her muffins. Lena's house was always immaculate, and today was no exception. After she dropped off her muffins downstairs, she took Finnegan for a long walk down by the river. The fresh air was invigorating, and she enjoyed the exercise.

When she got back, she realized she had left her phone at home and had messages from her mom, Clairese, and Jean Marc. Jean Marc asked her to call him.

Their conversation left her confused. There was no mention of the exchange last night; he was simply calling to confirm which day they were going to the farm.

"Do you want to come over tonight?" Hayden offered. "I will try and make up for last night."

"I can't, Doll face. I need to do some studying. I booked my trip to Montreal, by the way. Esme is pumped to see me."

Doll face? Well, it was better than Hayseed, I guess.

She told him she was on night shift for the next three nights, so she would be a bit out of commission. They discussed the plans for next weekend for the trip down to Willow Creek. They ended the conversation, but there was no 'I love you.'

Hayden sat and contemplated this. Maybe he was upset that *she* had not told him that she loved him yet.

Do you love him, Hayden? I think I do?

She spent the rest of the evening talking with her mom and then made a lunch date with Clairese.

The next two nights were brutally busy with sick patients, and Hayden came home from each shift exhausted. Louise was working in CCU for the three shifts and was on opposite breaks, so Hayden didn't see much of her.

Sunday night, Bernie and Jean Marc were both on duty—Bernie in ICU and Jean Marc in CCU. Hayden only saw them in passing at the beginning of the shift. The unit had settled down, and patients had stabilized considerably, so Jean Marc and Bernie were probably taking advantage of it and were studying or sleeping.

That night, Hayden was excited when Ally confided in her that she had met a new man! On their break together, Ally told her all the details.

"When you were in Willow Creek last weekend, Shaye had me over to her place for a wine night. Shaye's boyfriend came over and brought his roommate, and at the end of the night, he asked for my number. We have been on two dates already!"

"That is awesome, Ally. I am so happy for you!"

"How are things for you and Jean Marc?" Ally asked.

Before she could answer, Alana bounded over. "Who is up for breakfast this morning after these tortuous nights? I'm asking everyone, even the residents!"

Hayden initially said yes, but as the shift progressed, she developed a raging headache and a sore throat. By 6:00 a.m, she asked Peggy if she could go home.

Monday afternoon, Hayden awoke with a heavy cold and a fever. It was raining outside, and the forecast was bleak for the next few days. She stayed curled up in her bed for the next two days.

Jean Marc and Ally both texted her, asking if she needed anything. Lena had called her on Monday evening to tell her that Mrs. Adams had been admitted to the hospital for her high blood pressure. When she heard Hayden's congestion and raspy voice, she brought Hayden homemade chicken soup on Tuesday.

By Thursday, Hayden was feeling back to herself again. Just in time, as she and Jean Marc were headed to Willow Creek tomorrow to meet her family.

Jean Marc called her from the hospital. "Are you sure you are up for this?" he asked, adding, "I hope you aren't contagious anymore!"

Hayden assured him that she was better but then broke the news that they would be sleeping in separate bedrooms.

"You've got to be kidding!" he sputtered. "You are a grown woman! Do your parents think you don't have sex?"

"It's not like that, Jean Marc. My parents are just very traditional. Anyway, it is only for one night. I think you will survive."

"I was hoping we could 'get it on' on your single bed in your room!" he joked.

"Jean Marc!" she laughed halfheartedly.

The next afternoon, Jean Marc picked her up. Hayden was nervous but excited for him to see where she grew up and for him to meet her family.

She chattered excitedly as they drove out of the city. She pointed out the different crops and landmarks in the country as they drove. Then she directed him to turn off at the next secondary road, leading to her hometown.

"This long drive must get old for you every time you want to see your family," Jean Marc commented.

"Never," Hayden disagreed. "I love it, rain or shine. I love the country."

Jean Marc nodded in silence.

The Welcome sign loomed in the distance. Hayden kept her eyes glued straight ahead. She couldn't look at the cemetery as they passed.

"We can drive down Main Street, and then I will show you where I went to school too!" Hayden said happily.

They entered town, and Hayden directed him around and pointed out sights, including her high school. "Turn right here, and then we will start heading out to my family farm after you cross the train tracks."

"Well, what did you think?" Hayden squeezed Jean Marc's arm as he drove.

"Blink, and you'd miss it!" he laughed.

Hayden's face fell, and she looked straight ahead. Jean Marc looked over at her.

"Oh, come on, Hayseed, I was just teasing. Your town is great. I loved seeing where you went to school," he cajoled.

Hayden's head snapped over to look at him. "Can you stop calling me that? I really don't like it," she said coldly.

Jean Marc face recoiled, and he frowned. "Wow, what's got into you?"

Hayden stayed silent. Jean Marc rolled his eyes. "This is not a good way to start our weekend."

Hayden sighed. "We're going to turn onto the next Range Road there." She pointed out the window. "You might want to take it easy if you have never driven on gravel before."

Jean Marc maneuvered down the gravel road, but it was obvious he was not used to driving on gravel—the back end of his vehicle started to fishtail.

"Slow down, Jean Marc, or we will be in the ditch," she instructed. He listened this time and slowed the vehicle.

Hayden looked up the road and could see the dust billowing and a black truck approaching.

"Make sure you wave," she advised.

"Why?" he queried, "How can you tell this far back if it is someone you know?" he scoffed.

The truck had passed before Hayden could give an explanation. The driver of the black truck had raised his fingers off the wheel in a salutation, but Jean Marc had not reciprocated it. Hayden wanted to yell at him in frustration.

"It's just what we do," she said quietly. There was no point in getting mad over such a little thing. "You need to turn at the next Range Road." She tried to sound cheerier.

Soon enough, they were pulling into the yard of the Barrett Farm. "Nice sign," Jean Marc said brightly.

They parked and got out. Butch came over to greet them, and Hayden introduced them. She gave him his usual pat on the behind. "He's friendly," she invited.

"He's also all muddy," Jean Marc said, with an undertone of disgust.

They made their way to the entrance, and the front door opened.

"Sister!" greeted Paddy.

"Hi, Paddy. This is my friend, Jean Marc."

Jean Marc looked at Hayden in shock but then turned back to Paddy and nodded his head. "Good to meet you."

"Mom is downstairs getting pickles out of the cold room. I will tell her you are here!" Paddy volunteered and headed for the basement stairs.

Hayden turned to Jean Marc and smiled.

"Why didn't you tell me your brother is…I mean has Down Syndrome?" Jean Marc frowned.

"What difference would it make?" Hayden tilted her head in query.

"It just would have been nice to know," he whispered.

Winnie appeared from the basement with her arms loaded with two jars of pickles and a bottle of wine. "Hello, hello, you're here!"

Hayden hugged her mom. "Mom, this is Jean Marc Garrison, and Jean Marc, this is my mom, Winnie Barrett."

"Hey, good to meet you, Win!" Jean Marc nodded.

Hayden cringed. Her parents were very traditional. You called someone Mr. or Mrs. unless they directed you otherwise. She knew her mom would have said, "Please call me Winnie," but definitely not Win. As well, he did not shake her hand. What happened to his French charm?

Her mom was chatting with Jean Marc, offering him a drink. Hayden needed to tell him to be sure to shake her dad's hand! Her heart sank when the back door opened, and her dad walked in before she had the chance to whisper anything to him.

"Hello! You made it safe!" her dad said heartily.

"Hi, Dad. I'd like you to meet Jean Marc Garrison. Jean Marc, this is my dad, Cedric Barrett."

Jean Marc nodded. "Hey, Ced!"

Hayden saw her dad's eyes shoot briefly to her mom. Ced put out his hand, and then Jean Marc shook it.

Hayden couldn't look her dad in the eye.

Paddy was instructed to take Jean Marc's bags to the guest bedroom in the basement, and Jean Marc followed him, but not before looking back at Hayden and smirking about the sleeping arrangement.

Hayden busied herself helping her mom so that she didn't have to look her parents in the eye. Paddy and Jean Marc returned, and then they all sat in the front room. Ced and Jean Marc had a beer, and Hayden had a glass of wine; it helped calm her nerves.

Over supper, Hayden told her family about Louise and Bernie's engagement. Her Mom asked about all the arrangements.

"I think it is going to be quite the event," Jean Marc shared. "Bernie is from quite a well-to-do family, and Louise wants the big traditional event. I am Bernie's best man."

"Well, the youngest MacIntosh girl got married here a few weeks back, and they had over 200 people attend," Winnie shared.

"I don't want anything like that," Hayden said. "I think it is a huge expense, and you can do something much more simple and still have fun."

"Remember Shelby and Dean's wedding? They must have had over 160 people at Willow Creek Hall," her mom reminisced.

"Who are Shelby and Dean?" Jean Marc asked.

Hayden's heart went in her throat. Both her parents were staring at her. Even Paddy looked at her.

She swallowed hard. "She is my best friend here. We went to school together." She faltered. Now it was Jean Marc's turn to stare at her.

"Anyway, Louise and Bernie should have quite the event," Hayden said lightly, changing the direction of the conversation. "Louise is quite a planner; she has all the books."

There was a short silence. "Dinner was great, Win. Thank you." Jean Marc nodded in her direction, pushing his plate away.

Hayden got up and started clearing the dishes. She stood next to her mom in the kitchen, but there were no whispered accolades about her boyfriend. She didn't say anything about Shelby, either. Her silence was disquieting.

They all sat out on the porch after supper and dishes. Jean Marc and Ced talked about sports, and Hayden and her mom made small talk about the weather and the sunset. Hayden's stomach was in knots the whole evening. By 10:00 p.m, the mosquitos were out, so they all headed back in. Jean Marc kissed her on the cheek and retreated to the basement. Hayden feigned a headache and headed up to her room. Truthfully though, she did have a headache by the time she lay down on her bed. That night, she slept fitfully and dreamt of dancing in the flatbed of Wyatt's truck in the cornfield. But in the dream, she was in a wedding dress, and she was dancing with Jean Marc. He was drunk, and Hayden had to hold him up.

The next morning, she awoke to the smell of bacon and coffee. She had a quick shower and headed downstairs.

"I am sorry that I was not here to help, Mom. I am just getting over a cold, so I think I still needed the extra sleep."

"No worries, Hayden," her mom said brightly. Apparently, last night was in the past.

Hayden finished setting the table. Jean Marc emerged from the basement, showered, and outfitted in a collared dress shirt and jeans.

Hayden chuckled. "I guess I should have told you to bring old clothes for the farm."

Jean Marc shrugged and smiled. "All good. It's not like I am going to be driving the tractor or anything."

"Oh, you never know," joked Winnie. "Ced might put you to work here!"

Hayden heard the gator pull up. Looking out the window, she was surprised to see Paddy driving, with her dad in the front seat.

"Paddy is allowed to drive the gator now?" she asked.

"Oh, just a little bit around the yard, but occasionally Dad needs him to drive it out in the field."

Paddy and Ced came in shortly after, and they all had breakfast.

"Paddy, maybe you can help me show Jean Marc around the farm after breakfast and dishes?" Hayden suggested.

"Sure! I know where everything is, Hayden!" he grinned.

Winnie insisted she would clean up the dishes, so Hayden and Jean Marc headed outside, led by Paddy. They first went over to explore the barn. Jean Marc stepped in some manure and appeared annoyed that his shoes were dirty.

"I probably should have gotten you some rubber boots." Hayden apologized.

"Too late now," he snapped.

Paddy brought them over to the garden. He happily chatted about what each row was growing. Hayden was leaning down, pulling up weeds, when she noted Paddy stopped talking. She looked up to see Jean Marc reading something on his phone.

Paddy had stopped talking because he knew he was being ignored.

"Carry on, Paddy. I am listening," she encouraged.

"But I want Jean Marc to listen, too," he stammered.

Jean Marc looked up. "Oh, sorry, Paddy. You know I am a doctor, and I have very important emails about patients that I have to read." He spoke slowly, emphasizing each word. Hayden thought he sounded very patronizing.

"He's not two, Jean Marc. He just wants your attention," Hayden muttered under her breath.

Jean Marc slipped his phone back in his pocket.

Paddy finished his tour, and they walked back over to the barn. Ced pulled up in the gator.

"I've got a couple of cows I need to check on. Are you up for a ride out to the pasture, Jean Marc?" he invited.

"Oh, thanks, Ced, but I will pass. I am not really dressed for it. Seen one cow, you've seen 'em all!" Jean Marc laughed.

"Okay, no problem." Ced nodded with a thin smile.

"I'll come, Dad!" Paddy offered.

"Oh, I won't be long, son. You stay back here with Hayden and Jean Marc," Ced's eyes flickered to meet Hayden's briefly. She looked down; she couldn't bear to meet his look.

As they walked back to the house, Paddy asked to throw the ball with Jean Marc. Jean Marc hesitated and then glanced at Hayden, who looked at him pleadingly.

He sighed and replied with a minuscule of enthusiasm, "Sure, Paddy."

Hayden sat on the porch and watched them toss the ball back and forth. Winnie opened the porch door.

"Will you be staying for supper, Hayden?" she inquired.

Hayden turned to her mom and smiled. "Only if it is early, Mom, but please don't go to any fuss. I can help you too."

Minutes later, the ball-tossing was done. Paddy and Jean Marc came up the steps. They all retreated into the house as a cool wind had picked up.

"I can feel autumn in the air," Hayden announced. They joined Winnie in the front room.

"It will still be hot in Montreal for me next week." Jean Marc said as he pulled his phone back out of his pocket. "Twenty-eight degrees there right now." He frowned. "You sure have sketchy cell service here."

Winnie served dinner at 4:30 p.m, and Hayden and Jean Marc were on the road by 6:00 p.m. Hayden had never wanted to leave her home so badly in her life.

As they pulled away, Jean Marc patted her knee. "See? That was not so bad meeting the farm fam!"

Hayden forced a smile at him; then, they rode in silence for a few minutes. She feigned a sinus headache returning and said she wanted to sleep. She turned her head so he couldn't see the tears streaming down her face as they drove down that gravel road.

CHAPTER 15

Doubts

Monday morning came early, and Hayden was back on the day shift. As she pulled into the staff parking lot, she was surprised to see Jean Marc's red Bronco already parked in his usual spot. She headed into the ICU and her morning was busy with a familiar but unstable patient—Merle the Squirrel. Merle had been discharged from the ICU and then the hospital ward but had gone home and started abusing alcohol again. He returned to ICU with a gastrointestinal bleed. This time, he was intubated, heavily sedated, and on medications to control the bleeding and support his blood pressure. Hayden began her hectic morning administering a blood transfusion as well.

When her nurse clinician, Peggy, made her rounds, Hayden voiced her concerns that Merle didn't have enough IV access for all his medications and blood transfusions. She suggested that a central venous catheter (in a large vein above the heart or in his neck) should be considered for Merle. Peggy agreed and said she would discuss it in doctors' rounds or at least with the resident, Dr. Tina Chan, who was on duty today.

Both Hayden and her colleague Jonas in the next room over were very busy with their patients, so neither could relieve each other for a coffee break. It was 9:30 a.m, and Hayden's stomach was growling. Just then, Jean Marc popped his head in her patient's room as she was changing one of her medication bags.

"Hey, gorgeous, I brought you a tea and a scone from the coffee shop. I know that they won't be as good as Lena's, but what can I say?"

Hayden's face lit up. "That is so thoughtful! Thank you, I am starved!"

"I will leave them out here on your workstation. Talk to you later." He winked at her and left the room.

Wow, thought Hayden. *Maybe I am being too hard on him.*

She finished changing her medication bag. Taking a deep breath, she realized she was finally caught up with her work. Just then, Jonas came into the room.

"I am sorry I have not been able to help you, Hayden. I have had a crazy morning!" he apologized.

"Not to worry, Jonas, I have too. Are you ready to go for a break?"

"Well, I had breakfast before I came, so if you would like to go first, you can. I see someone special brought you a treat." He smiled and gestured towards her tea and packaged scone on her workstation.

Hayden blushed. "Yeah, that was sweet of him." She took Jonas up on his offer to let her go for break first. She gave him a report on her patient and then headed to the staff break room and appreciatively sat down to eat her snack.

Just then, Louise emerged out of the staff washroom. "Oh, hi, Hayden. You are just coming for break now? You must be having a busy morning!"

"Yes, both Jonas and I have been super busy. Jean Marc was sweet enough to drop this off for me." She gratefully took a bite of her scone.

"How sweet," she said, putting her left hand to her heart, perhaps letting it linger there so Hayden could see her ring?

"Listen, Hayden. I know you will probably want to organize a unit wedding shower for me. I want," she cleared her throat, "I mean *Bernie and I* want everyone to know the places that we are registering for gifts. How about I email you a list?"

Hayden almost choked on her scone. First of all, it was very dry. The second reason was she could not believe the audacity of Louise's request. She was almost too stunned to say anything.

"Oh, um, sure, I guess, Louise." She stared at her for a moment. *Doesn't the wedding party usually plan that?* she thought to herself.

"How are the plans coming along? Have you set a date yet? Picked your wedding party, stuff like that?" Hayden inquired.

"We are pretty sure it will be this coming July. We are just looking at venues. That will give us nearly ten months to pull it all together! Anyway, I've got to get back to CCU. I will email you that list, okay?"

Hayden nodded and turned back to her dry scone and tea. *Yeah, I'll get right on that, Louise,* she thought sarcastically.

Hayden shortened her break and went back so Jonas could go. Doctors' rounds were just approaching her room with the group of residents. Bernie smiled at her, and Jean Marc winked.

Hayden started her report about Merle when suddenly, all the pagers went off, and a code blue was called overhead. Jean Marc and another resident quickly left the unit. Hayden was not on the code team today; her patient was too sick. Bernie and Tina stayed back to finish rounds.

Dr. Tina Chan agreed to come in and insert the central line for Hayden's patient, Merle. Hayden liked Tina; she was very bright, personable, and adept with her skills. They chatted as Tina expertly inserted the line in Merle's neck.

"This rotation is almost over for you all. Two more weeks! Where do you go next?" Hayden asked.

"Well, I am an R3, and I am going to L&D next. That is what I plan to specialize in." Even though Tina was wearing a mask, Hayden could detect her smile under her mask.

The number behind the R (Resident) meant what year they were in their residency. L&D meant labor and delivery.

"Jean Marc is an R4, right?" Tina queried as she stitched the line in place.

"Yes, he is. Bernie is too. Jean Marc goes to internal medicine next and Bernie to anesthesia."

"Right!" Tina agreed. She removed the sterile drapes from where she was working. "I think I am all done here, Hayden. If you don't mind calling for a portable chest X-ray to verify placement, that would be great."

Capathia leaned into the room. "Hi, Tina. We just got back from the code, and the patient is in CCU. I would really appreciate your help over there. My resident is struggling."

Capathia was the nurse clinician on duty in CCU today. Peggy was in ICU.

"How was the code?" Hayden asked Capathia as Tina walked out.

"It was fine. Thank goodness Jean Marc was there because the beetle head I have on in CCU today doesn't know his ass from his elbow. I am fixin' to…well, never mind. You have yourself a smart boyfriend there, Hayden."

Hayden just smiled as she placed the sterile dressing on Merle's new central line.

After her shift, Hayden went home. It was the last week of August, and you could definitely feel the crispness in the air once the evening approached. She said hello to Lena and then took Finnegan for a quick walk. When she returned, she was surprised to see Jean Marc pulling up.

"I tried to text you," he said as he got out of his vehicle.

"Sorry, I forgot my phone at home." She returned Finnegan to Lena, who invited her in, but she told her Jean Marc had just come by.

Down in her place, Jean Marc was waiting with Chinese takeout for her. Jean Marc hated it but knew she loved it.

"Wow, you are spoiling me today!"

Jean Marc stayed for the evening, which ended with a rendezvous on her couch, which to her pleasant surprise, was enjoyable and satisfying.

"I'm going to miss you in Montreal," he said as they hugged goodbye.

"I know. I wish that I could have come! Will I see you tomorrow before you go?" she posed.

"You may see me on the unit, but Bernie is driving me to the airport in the afternoon. I'll send you my flight information, so maybe you can pick me up when I get back?"

Hayden agreed to this, and they said goodnight.

The next day, they did not see each other on the unit. Hayden had a reasonable shift and went home and watched a movie. Just as it was ending, her phone buzzed.

Are we still on for lunch tomorrow? C ☺

She had almost forgotten about her lunch date with Clairese! She texted back that she was looking forward to it and headed to bed.

The next day at noon, Clairese and Hayden met at a great little sandwich place. Even though it was a fair walking distance from her place, Hayden enjoyed the jaunt, as it was a beautiful sunny day. She wanted to savor what was left of the summer.

They sat out on the patio, and Clairese ordered margaritas for them both. They talked about Clairese's new place and garden, their work, and Clairese's new relationship. She was dating a police officer that had brought a psychiatric patient into the emergency one night. It was early in the relationship, but she was optimistic. Then she asked Hayden about Jean Marc.

"It is good," Hayden said as she took a drink from her margarita, not looking Clairese in the eyes.

"Spill the beans, girl! I can read right through you! How was the visit back home?"

Hayden relayed the events of the visit to the farm.

"It is hard when you come from two different backgrounds." Clairese nodded in understanding.

The margarita may have let Hayden's guard down, and she shared her disappointment in their intimacy.

"It sounds as though all he is ever concerned about is getting his rocks off," Clairese said contemptuously. "What an egotistical prick."

As Hayden walked back home later, the effects of the margarita wore off, and she regretted saying so much. When she got back home, she texted Clairese, who assured her of the confidentiality of *all* of their conversation. She was relieved.

That evening, she called her mom, and they had a nice chat. Her dad and Paddy were out in the pasture, so she didn't get to talk to them. During the conversation, Jean Marc, or their visit to the farm, was not brought up. She thought Winnie might have said *something*, but the silence about him was deafening. Hayden had never brought any other man home to meet her parents besides Wyatt.

Hayden's shift the next day was much more reasonable. Her patient, Merle, was much more hemodynamically stable. However, Jonas was busy again with his trauma patient. After Hayden had assessed and turned Merle, as well as documented everything, she popped over to help Jonas with his patient.

"Hey, can I give you a hand with anything, Jonas?"

"Oh, I would appreciate it, Miss Hayden. Thank you so much!" Jonas smiled earnestly. Jonas was a respectful person and was always appreciative of any assistance.

Jonas asked Hayden to change some of the IV tubing and, if she could, help him with a dressing change.

Jonas' patient was mechanically ventilated and heavily sedated. He was in spinal precautions with a cervical collar in place and had multiple fractures. When turning him, he required a 'log roll' to make sure that his whole spine remained in perfect alignment when he was turned. He had some spinal fractures, and turning him incorrectly could result in damage to his spinal cord and possibly paralysis.

"What is the story on this guy?" Hayden asked quietly as they changed the dressing together.

"He was the driver of a vehicle involved in a MVC. His passenger was not restrained and was ejected. He was deceased on the scene." Jonas said sadly, whispering the last sentence.

It should have been me that died. Chunk's words echoed in her head.

Hayden and Jonas finished the dressing change. "I need to turn him, and he is a log roll. Can you take the head? I will call some others to help us as well." Jonas requested.

Hayden positioned herself at the head of the bed and placed her forearms on either side of the patient's head and neck brace. Her thumbs rested on the man's collarbones and her fingers behind the patient's neck. As the person at the head of the bed, it was Hayden's responsibility to coordinate the roll and count aloud so that everyone was aware of when to roll the patient.

Ally, Betty, and Alana came in to help. The man was quite large, so it was good to have all the help. When they turned him, Jonas was going to auscultate his lungs with his stethoscope, assess the man's backside, and rub some lotion on his skin.

"My patient here has a C3 C4 fracture, so strict spinal precautions everyone," Jonas instructed.

Everyone positioned themselves.

"Mr. Evans, we are going to turn you on your left side," Jonas warned his patient. "Your call Hayden."

"Okay, everyone ready? One, two, three." Hayden called out, and they rolled.

"Nasty fractures." Ally whispered to everyone. She knew that even unconscious and sedated patients may still be aware and hear what health care professionals are saying over top of them.

"C3 C4 fractures, did you say, Jonas?" Alana asked quietly.

"Yes, from a big MVC." Jonas clarified. "Okay, I am done. Hayden, are you ready to roll back?"

You know they said I am probably responsible for his death. I wasn't wearing a seatbelt, so my big drunk body here, tossed around in the truck and probably hit him. Broke his neck or something worse.

"Hayden?"

"Oh, I am sorry, guys! Sure. Ready? One, two, three." They laid the patient flat.

"You okay, Hayden? Ally touched Hayden's arm.

"Yeah, I'm good." She went and sat back at her workstation. *Are you sure about that, Hayden? Autumn is approaching.*

CHAPTER 16

An Autumn Tragedy

The summer following Hayden's second year of nursing training was a great one. She and Wyatt had been doing the long-distance relationship thing for two years now, and it worked for both of them. Lethbridge was only just over an hour away from Willow Creek, so they saw each other almost every weekend. During the week, she was busy with school and clinical, and Wyatt was working on his parent's farm, for which his parents paid him. He had saved some money and had purchased some land of his own as well. On the side, he was taking some online business courses.

Hayden's classmates had gotten to know Wyatt, so he was a regular fixture at any weekend parties. Hayden was not a huge partygoer, but she did enjoy some events, especially since it gave her the opportunity to meet new friends on campus. Wyatt had asked her on a couple of occasions if she thought being in a relationship with him was "cramping her style" and if she wanted to date others. She always assured him that she was one-hundred percent happy with their relationship.

In the summer months, if Wyatt wasn't busy working on his own family farm, he was at Hayden's place. They tried to spend as much time as possible together. They would hang out with Paddy or help Winnie and Ced with the garden or the cattle.

At the beginning of August, there was an annual three-day event in Willow Springs called 'Back to our Roots.' The kickoff was a little parade in town on the Friday morning, which was always well attended. There was a mini midway with multiple food concessions, a beer garden, and a family barn dance on the Saturday night. The evenings always ended with fireworks as well.

'Back to Our Roots' was fundamental for embracing the community spirit. There was a large tent set up for locals to display (and sell) their artwork and handicrafts. Another tent had exhibitors for a fun and friendly produce competition: the biggest and best vegetables and fruit. Wyatt and Shelby's mom, June, always entered several of her vegetables, but she also had a booth set up to sell her pickled cucumbers, carrots, beans and beets. Shelby and Dean and Wyatt and Hayden took turns helping out at the booth. It was always a fun time.

That summer, they went to some country music festivals, and they went camping several times with Shelby and Dean, as well as Chunk and his girlfriend of two years, Gena. Her full name was Imogene, and she hated the nickname Genie, so everyone called her Gena. Gena was a year younger than Shelby and Hayden but had gone to high school with them. She was quiet and shy, a contrast to Chunk, who was gregarious and funny. She always called him by his given name of Dylan, but everyone else called him Chunk. It was evident that she adored Chunk, but he always appeared to take her for granted. Who knew what they were like when they were alone?

It was the September long weekend, and the six of them decided to have one more camping weekend before Hayden headed back to school. She was entering her third year of nursing training. The first two years had been at Lethbridge College; her last two would be spent at the University of Lethbridge.

The six of them met out at the Writing-on-Stone Provincial Park Campground, which is a UNESCO World Heritage Site. It is an hour south of Lethbridge and situated on the Milk River. Sandstone outcrops (that have been eroded by ice and wind) called hoodoos surround the area. At the park, there are over fifty petroglyphs. The six spent the weekend touring, hiking and then canoeing down the Milk River. The evenings were spent around the fire, with Chunk providing most of the entertainment with funny stories and imitations.

Monday morning, they were packing up their site. Hayden was anxious to get back to the farm as tomorrow, Ced and Wyatt were helping her move into her own apartment in Lethbridge. For the last two years, she had lived on campus at the College in a dorm.

"God damn it!" Wyatt exclaimed as Hayden carried their cooler over to the truck.

"What's wrong?" she asked, concerned.

"This truck will not start, AGAIN!" Wyatt huffed in exasperation.

"You are lucky we have not left yet, bro!" Chunk laughed.

Shelby and Dean had already packed up and left half an hour ago. Chunk pulled his truck over, and using jumper cables; they got the truck running again.

Chunk and Gena followed them on the highway back to Willow Creek to ensure they got back safely.

"We're going to have to ask your dad to drive his truck tomorrow, Hayden. This piece of junk is so unreliable," Wyatt said, shaking his head.

Once she was settled in her new apartment, September flew by as Hayden was immersed in her studies. Wyatt was working long days and evenings during harvest, helping his dad combine their grain. That resulted in them only talking on the phone, instead of seeing each other on the weekends. Sometimes they even talked while he was in the combine, late into the evening.

Thanksgiving weekend was the first weekend they saw each other, but it was also filled with visiting and celebrating with family. The following Thursday, Wyatt called Hayden in Lethbridge.

"Do you think you can come home this weekend?" he asked, with an undertone of excitement in his voice.

"Why, what's up?" she asked suspiciously.

"Well, the forecast is for rain all weekend, so I won't be harvesting. Brad and Elise are going to be hosting an Oktoberfest party, and I thought it would be fun to go to."

"I have a big pharmacology exam next week, Wyatt." sighed Hayden. "Why don't you come down here?"

Hayden was not fond of Elise, and she knew that Shelby and Dean would not be there. She had just gotten off the phone with Shelby before speaking with Wyatt. They were going to be attending a wedding this weekend out of town.

"Come on, Sweetness. I am sure Paddy and your mom and dad would like to see you too."

She suspected Wyatt was up to something, and she really missed him, so she relented.

"All right. I will be there Saturday morning."

"If you need to study, you can use my body," Wyatt suggested in his most seductive tone.

"I am studying for pharmacology, not anatomy, you goof!" Hayden laughed.

Saturday morning, Hayden arrived home. In retrospect, she was glad that Wyatt had convinced her to come. The countryside colors of red, orange, and yellow were even more stunning this weekend than last. As she drove into the entrance to the farm, she noted her mom had set up pumpkins, a scarecrow, and a bale of hay next to their family welcome sign.

She texted Wyatt and invited him for supper for 5:00 p.m. He said he would be there. After lunch, she went for a walk with Paddy and Butch down the gravel road, which had not been a wise idea, as the sky opened up and they had to run back home. They were soaking wet by the time they entered the back porch.

At 4:30, she was in the living room studying when she heard a truck pull into the drive. She looked out the window but didn't recognize the grey Ford F150. She was surprised when she watched Wyatt emerge from the driver's door.

She threw on her rubber boots and ran out. Thankfully, the rain had let up.

"What's this?" she yelled with excitement.

"Surprise, Sweetness! How do you like it?" Wyatt stood in front of the truck. Smiling proudly, dressed in a plaid shirt, jeans and cowboy boots, Hayden thought he never looked more attractive.

"I wondered why you were acting so suspicious!" She threw her arms around him, and he kissed her fervidly.

Just then, Ced emerged from the garage with Paddy.

"Well, what do we have here?" he chuckled.

Wyatt excitedly showed both Paddy and Ced around the truck, explaining all the features. They lifted the hood and talked about the engine. Hayden had hopped inside the driver's seat. It still smelled new inside, even though it was two years old, Wyatt had said.

Winnie came out and hugged Wyatt. "Very nice choice, Wyatt. I like the color."

"It is gunpowder grey," he said proudly.

It started to drizzle again, and it was suppertime, so they headed inside. After eating, Hayden and Wyatt headed to the party in town. Being October, it was getting dark so much sooner.

As they drove down the road, Wyatt seemed fidgety. Within minutes, he pulled off at a turn-out access to a field.

"What are you doing?" Hayden asked.

"Don't you recognize this field?" Wyatt laughed as he turned and removed his seatbelt.

"No, should I?"

Wyatt leaned into the back seat and pulled out a triangular-shaped bouquet wrapping. "This is the field we danced in after

Shelby and Dean's wedding." He reminded her. He handed her the bouquet wrapping.

"Right!" she remembered. Hayden opened it, and inside were four roses.

"Well, I wanted to take you to our special creek spot, but it was too damn muddy, so I thought this was a good second contender. There are four roses there for the four years we have been together."

Hayden's heart started to race. *Was he going to ask me to marry him?*

Wyatt took a deep breath. "I just wanted to say that now that I have purchased some land and this truck, and I am getting my business courses done…." Wyatt swallowed. "Well, the next thing is, I want to start saving for a ring for you, Hayden. And of course, I want to make sure it is exactly the one that you want."

Hayden undid her seatbelt and leaned over to him. They kissed and embraced. "I am sure whatever you choose will be perfect, Wyatt."

"That is great. I am not going to ask you formally until I have your ring. And I sure as hell ain't going to ask you here in a muddy cornfield," he laughed. "Especially that cocksucker, Doug Kendrick's field!"

They both laughed.

"I just don't know where we are going to live once we get married. I guess we could purchase a mobile home and put it on my land. We would have to get services out there, though," Wyatt surmised.

Hayden sat up. "Wyatt, I don't think it's a good idea to get married until I am done school. Plus, I would like to work in Calgary for a couple of years and get some experience in a tertiary hospital before I came out to work in the little hospital here in Willow Creek."

Wyatt looked shocked and went very quiet.

"It would only be a couple of years, Wyatt. There is no rush." Hayden reassured him.

"Okay," he replied, looking down. "I guess we have some talking and planning to do then." He looked at his watch and then said, "We better go."

Hayden put her hand on his arm. "We don't have to go to the party, Wyatt. Maybe we should just stay here and talk."

"No, I told Brad and Elise we were coming," he said abruptly as he pulled his seatbelt back on and restarted the truck.

They drove the rest of the way in silence.

When they arrived at the party, it was well underway. They had a keg of beer, and some people were dressed in Oktoberfest outfits. It was loud, and everyone appeared to be having a good time.

"Hi, guys!" Elise greeted them as they walked in. "There is sauerkraut and sausages in the kitchen. Please help yourself!'

Brad and Wyatt clapped each other on the back in an embrace. Hayden looked around the room. She surprisingly did not know a lot of the people at the party, as they were more Wyatt's age group. She probably knew some of their siblings.

She reluctantly grabbed a beer (she hated beer). "Do you want to drink, and I will be the designated driver?" Hayden offered Wyatt as he chatted with Brad.

He looked at her, and despite the jovial atmosphere, there just seemed to be sadness in his eyes. "No, I'm good."

Hayden felt out of place at the party and wished that Shelby and Dean or Chunk and Gena had come. Just as that thought crossed her mind, Chunk came staggering around the corner, clearly intoxicated.

"Bro!" he yelled, grabbing Wyatt in an embrace. Wyatt looked back at Hayden with an uneasy look.

"Hey, Chunk. Where is Gena tonight?" Hayden asked.

"She dumped me this afternoon. Two years together, and it is ALL over," he slurred, punching his beer in the air and spilling a bit in the process. "Apparently, she says I drink too much! I need a girlfriend, not a nagging mother!" he said, looking at them both for affirmation.

Hayden and Wyatt exchanged a concerned look.

"How did it go tonight, Bro? You know, with the truck and roses!" Chunk winked at Wyatt.

"All good," Wyatt said quietly, looking away.

Hayden knew that they were best friends, so she was not entirely surprised that Wyatt had told Chunk his plans.

"Well, that's no ringin' endorsement!" he said, his voice getting louder.

"Chunk..." Hayden quelled him.

"Hayden wants to finish school first and then work in Calgary for a couple of years first." Wyatt shrugged. "It will all work out."

Chunk stared at them both in surprising silence and then yelled, "We need another drink! Come on, friends!"

People started staring at Chunk.

Hayden looked nervously at Wyatt. "I think we should take him home. Did he drive here?"

"Brad already took his keys," a guy standing close by advised.

"Hey, Buddy, why don't I drive you home? Let's go for a drive in my new truck." Wyatt encouraged.

Wyatt, Hayden, and Chunk left the party, not even saying goodbye to Brad and Elise. There were so many people; only those standing by them noticed them leave.

"You hurl in my truck, Chunk, and I will have to fucking kill you," Wyatt warned.

"I'm good, Bro. You know me, I don't puke often," Chunk said more calmly.

"I'll drive you home first, okay?" Wyatt offered to Hayden as they all climbed into the truck. Chunk climbed into the back seat, and Hayden sat in the front.

"Are you sure?" Hayden said nervously, "You won't need help with getting him in his house?"

"I'll call his brother if I have to," Wyatt said as they started to drive.

"I'm fine, guys!" Chunk assured them.

They drove in silence, with only the radio playing.

"I am really sorry, guys. I guess I am just broken up over my girl," Chunk mumbled from the back seat. Then, he laid his head back and was asleep in seconds.

The rain began again in vengeance as they neared the Barrett Ranch. As they pulled in, Hayden gathered her roses from behind the seat.

"Are you sure you are okay with him?" Hayden asked Wyatt.

"All good, Sweetness. I will call you tomorrow."

Hayden stared in the dark from the passenger seat over at Wyatt.

"We can talk more about this tomorrow." she offered. Wyatt nodded and smiled. She could see the outline of his thick, curly black hair in the glow from the yard light.

"I love you," she said sincerely.

"I love you too, Hayden."

She hesitated but then got out of the truck. She ran onto the porch to avoid getting drenched again.

That was the last time she ever saw Wyatt. The RCMP came to her house at 6:00 a.m the next morning. She could hear her mom sobbing from downstairs when her dad woke her up to tell her. Chunk had been flown by helicopter to Calgary and was in the ICU for the next two weeks. Wyatt had died in the rollover at the scene.

CHAPTER 17

Annoyances

The next morning at work, Peggy introduced two new nurses who were orientating to the unit. Eric, an older fellow with previous ICU experience in another city, who was orientating with Jonas; and Kennedy, a newer nurse, who Louise was orientating. Everyone welcomed them both.

"Don't worry, Kennedy. I will show you the ropes!" Louise chortled and patted Kennedy's hand. Kennedy looked terrified.

Ally rolled her eyes at Hayden. Hayden wanted to yell at Louise. *How fucking condescending!*

"Oh, and by the way, everyone, next Friday is this group of residents' last shift. I have organized a super fun night at a piano bar down on 17th Avenue, and everyone is welcome!" Louise clapped her hands together once.

Peggy and Capathia gave out the assignments, and everyone headed into the ICU or CCU for their bedside patient reports. Capathia was covering for Carl today.

Hayden had a steady shift. Lunch approached, and she headed into the staff room. Louise and Kennedy were sitting at the table, and Louise abruptly stopped talking as Hayden entered. They both looked away and focused on their lunch.

Okay, obviously talking about me. Hayden sat over on the couch, ate her lunch, and read on her phone.

That evening as she drove home, her alley was blocked off as the city was repairing some big potholes. She had to park in front, on the street. As she got out of her car, she looked across the street to see someone sitting in their vehicle, staring at her but then they quickly looked away. She turned to grab her belongings in the back seat and turned back to look, just in time to see the individual pull away in their vehicle. Bile rose in her throat when she realized it was Larry's friend, Jezz. She didn't see Larry around.

Hayden was a bit unnerved but did her best to settle in for a relaxing night. She made some popcorn and turned on some music. She sat down on her couch to look at her mail. She opened her visa bill to see the $1000.00 deposit for the trip. No one had paid her yet, and frankly, she wasn't sure she wanted to go on a trip with Louise anymore.

She texted Jean Marc, who told her he made it safely to Montreal and was having a great time with Esme. He also said that Bernie offered to pick him up at the airport when he returned. She shrugged when she read his text.

The rest of her week involved some clothes shopping, vacuuming, and cleaning her place and walks down by the river with Finnegan. Lena was grateful, as she said she had not been feeling well this week. Hayden sensed she was sad again and hoped that it did not involve Larry.

Communication from Jean Marc this week was scarce, but she assumed he was busy with family and friends. He would be back in two more days. She focused on her next three shifts at work. Louise was cordial with her, but she was very distant. Bernie was on duty for Hayden's last shift, and he was very pleasant and chatty with her. She still felt awkward about asking for money for the trip and thought she would deal with it when Jean Marc returned.

On late Monday night, Jean Marc returned, and as offered, Bernie picked him up at the airport. He texted Hayden to say that he would come by and see her after his shift on Tuesday. She was excited to see him but reminded him that she had to work the day shift on Wednesday, Thursday, and Friday.

Tuesday evening, Hayden had a long bubble bath and took some extra time to do her hair. She wore a new shirt and jeans that she thought complimented her figure. By 9:30 p.m, Jean Marc had not called or texted her. She was a bit annoyed but realized he could have been caught up with an unstable patient or a Code Blue.

At 10:00 p.m, there was a soft rap on her door. She was half asleep on her couch, and it startled her. She looked out to see Jean Marc at the top of the stairs.

"I'm so sorry!" he said, handing her some flowers. "I ended up going home, and Louise had cooked some pasta for Bernie, and they invited me to have a bite. I had a glass of wine and lost track of the time!"

They embraced, and Hayden thought skeptically, *a glass of wine? Smells like more.*

"I know you have to work tomorrow, so I won't stay long. I just wanted to see you."

They cuddled on the couch, and he told her about his trip to Montreal and all the things he did with his sister Esme and also his mom, who joined them for a few days. By 11:30, Hayden's eyes were drooping, and she was suppressing her yawns.

"Let's pick this up tomorrow night," he said, caressing her breasts.

"Okay, I am so sorry!" apologized Hayden. "Oh, you know about this piano bar party for Friday that Louise is planning?"

"Yup, should be fun! I will see you on the unit tomorrow." He kissed her goodbye.

For the next three day shifts, Hayden was in charge. Peggy was on vacation, and she left a note for Hayden, "*This will be great practice for you if you decide to apply for my position*!" Hayden was happy to be in charge but also disappointed. Being in charge often meant staying late after your shift to give a report. Carl (Snarl) was the clinician on for CCU, and Hayden did her best to avoid him.

On Wednesday, there was a code at the end of the shift, so Jean Marc was late leaving. Thursday, he had meetings at the end of the day for the end of his ICU/CCU rotation. So, they did not see each other for either evening.

"I guess I will see you Friday at the *Piano Bar* then!" Hayden said on the phone to him Thursday.

Friday, Hayden was late leaving the unit as the new nurse, Kennedy, had a bit of a melt down after her shift. After debriefing with her, Hayden headed out to her car to find it wouldn't start. She called Jean Marc on his cell to see if he could swing back from the bar to get her. However, when she started talking to him, it was obvious he had already had too much to drink.

"Just take an Uber!" he suggested, the music loud, with laughter in the background.

She elected to call a tow truck, which came and jumped her battery after she waited an additional forty-five minutes at the hospital. She drove home, intending to change out of her scrubs and then head over to the *Piano Bar.* By the time she got home, it was 10:00 p.m, and it was raining. She was annoyed and had lost all interest in going. She texted both Ally and Jean Marc, saying she wasn't coming. She changed into her pajamas, turned off her phone, and went to bed.

In the morning, she turned her phone back on. There were multiple texts from people last night, attempting to cajole her into changing her mind and coming down to the bar. She shrugged, deleted them, and then turned her phone back off for the rest of the day.

CHAPTER 18

Jonas' Secret

Autumn was approaching, but Hayden was determined to avoid spiraling into a depression. Since Wyatt's death, autumn was always a difficult season to face, but counseling had reinforced that going forward, she needed to make new happy memories for the season. *This could help change how you feel about the autumn season when it approaches every year,* her counselor had said.

She didn't hear from Jean Marc all Saturday, although she did have her phone turned off. Instead, she helped Lena in the garden prepare for fall as the cool nights had already started turning the leaves yellow, and some leaves had even started to fall. Sunday morning, Hayden was still in her pajamas, reading the news on her phone, when she heard a tap on her door. She looked out to see Jean Marc. When she opened the door, she was surprised to see him standing there with two steaming teas from the *Bean Scene.*

"Good morning!" he smiled, handing her a tea.

He apologized for Friday night and told her that everyone had missed her at the party. Nothing was said about yesterday, but she assumed he was probably sleeping off a hangover.

She got dressed, and they headed over to the local farmer's market and then went for brunch at a great pub close by. They talked about Jean Marc's new rotation in internal medicine. He expressed apprehension, as he heard from classmates that it usually resulted in long hours with consults in emergency, or lengthy investigations with patients on units fifty-five and fifty-six. The patients often had a grocery list of complex medical issues.

They headed back to Hayden's and spent the rest of the evening in her bed. Jean Marc made an extra effort to be attentive to her needs, rather than just his. He even spent the night, which was a rarity.

Monday evening, they met Bernie and Louise for pizza. Louise chattered away about the wedding plans with Hayden, and there did not seem to be any distance between them at all. Hayden mentioned to them all that her Visa bill had come in for the deposit on the trip. They all agreed to e-transfer her money soon.

Tuesday was the beginning of the new rotation for Jean Marc, but that also meant a new group of residents for the ICU and CCU. Hayden was on the night shift for the next two nights in the CCU, and thankfully, they were reasonable nights. She was lucky to have Ally working with her.

"I see that Louise and Kennedy have become fast friends." Ally said, lifting her eyebrows. They sat behind the central monitors, watching all their patient's heart rhythms on the big screens.

Hayden shrugged and told her about the pizza night and that everything had seemed fine between them. "However, here at work, she is distant. I just let it roll off my back."

Ally and Hayden made plans to go out for lunch on Friday. Hayden was thinking of driving down to Willow Creek for Saturday and Sunday, as Jean Marc was on call the whole weekend, so it would be unlikely that she would see much of him.

"I was going to tell you this at lunch on Friday, but I can't wait anymore!" confided Ally. "Liam and I decided to take the plunge and move in together…except that he got a job in Edmonton, so I am moving." Ally smiled, but it was a mixture of happiness but also sadness.

"Oh my gosh, Ally! I am so happy for you! I mean, I will miss you desperately, but that is so exciting!" Hayden hugged Ally.

"It won't be until the end of November, but it is going to come quick."

The weekend arrived. Hayden ended up taking her car in for service Saturday, so her plans to go home were pushed to another weekend. She spent the rest of the weekend reading a book, paying bills, and doing some laundry.

Monday arrived, and it was back to the night shift. Hayden had texted Jean Marc through the week, but his reply and communication were sparse. She knew he was busy in his new rotation, but she was still a bit surprised.

Entering the break room on Monday night was even more of a surprise. Displayed on the staff communication board was a poster inviting everyone to a wedding shower for Louise, hosted by *Maid of Honor*, Kennedy! Louise would not make eye contact with Hayden. Even sullen Danni gave a questioning look and shrug to Hayden.

"It is going to be a fun time, so I hope you all can come!" gushed Kennedy.

Fill your boots, Kennedy, thought Hayden.

In the morning, after her shift, Hayden walked wearily out to her car. She was surprised not to see Jean Marc's vehicle parked in his usual spot.

On her next night shift, Hayden was looking after a very ill patient with septic shock. He was on multiple medications to support his blood pressure, continuous dialysis to support his failing kidneys, and was, of course, mechanically ventilated on a machine. It resulted in a very demanding and hectic shift. Hayden had to stay a bit late after her shift to finish her documentation. As she was heading towards the front entrance to leave, she saw Jean Marc coming out of the hospital café with a colleague, having both just grabbed coffees.

"Good morning!" Jean Marc smiled with those eyes." You are leaving late."

"Sick patient I was dealing with all night. I am exhausted. How are you guys?" she smiled wearily.

Just then, Jean Marc's colleague, Dr. Harry Gurinder received a page. "Excuse me. I must answer this. I will meet you upstairs."

Hayden turned to Jean Marc. "Hey, I didn't see your car in the lot?"

"Yeah, I caught a ride with Bernie. Did you get your car serviced on the weekend?"

"I did. But I am working nights all weekend, so I won't be going home for a while," she shrugged.

"I am sorry that we have not seen each other much. This rotation is even heavier than I anticipated. I should run and catch up with Harry. Talk soon, okay?" Jean Marc winked. Hayden was well aware, no public displays of affection!

The week went by quickly with the three night shifts. Next week, she wanted to plan some things with friends on her days off. Maybe she would text Clairese.

Sunday night, Hayden entered the break room 'with pleasure.' Her dad always told her that she could go to work 'with pleasure' on her last shift, as she anticipated her days off ahead. She had just been approved tonight for a day off next week, so she was looking forward to a stretch of four days off. It was an even more pleasurable shift, as Louise was off ill tonight. Kennedy looked terrified sitting there without her 'ringmaster.'

Hayden had a very stable ICU patient tonight who was awaiting transfer to the inpatient floor. She would be relieving for break with Jonas tonight.

"If you need any help tonight, Jonas, I am more than willing. My patient is very stable," Hayden offered.

Jonas looked up from his charting. "Oh, thank you, Miss Hayden." He looked uncomfortable and then quickly looked away. Hayden had caught him staring at her during report. He had quickly looked away then too when they had made eye contact.

What's with him?

Hayden had finished her documentation when Shaye asked for her help to initiate an intravenous infusion on her patient.

"I've tried twice, and her veins just roll. I know you are the IV queen!" Shaye laughed.

Hayden took her time and was successful in obtaining the IV access and was taping it in place.

"So, what do you think of this wedding shower thing with Louise?" Shaye asked as she attached the IV medication tubing to the new IV Hayden started.

Hayden just shrugged. "I don't know. I kind of feel bad that I had not organized it yet, but truthfully, since Kennedy is the maid of honor, she rightfully should be the one organizing it."

"Is that still politically correct, the maid of honor title? I am surprised that Kennedy endorsed that. She told me she is lesbian and that she hates certain designations, so I thought she would not want that *title*," Shaye surmised.

"Really? I didn't know that about her," Hayden shrugged again.

Hayden headed back to her workstation. Not being busy made the night drag on. She again offered her assistance to Jonas.

"Actually, Miss Hayden, yes. Can you help me change my patient's abdominal dressing?" Jonas said nervously and then looked away.

This time, Hayden stared at him. Something *was* up.

Hayden checked on her patient as Jonas gathered his supplies for the dressing change. When Hayden entered the room, he shut the sliding glass doors. That was unusual. Hayden was now intrigued.

As they began the dressing change, Jonas chatted nervously about the patient's wound and what he was doing. Then he dropped the bomb.

"Miss Hayden, you know my wife is a nurse up on unit fifty-five? Yes, she really likes it, and well, she has met you, and she really likes you and knows about our family and friends here in the ICU." He rambled nervously.

"Jonas," Hayden put her hand on his arm, "if you have something important to tell me, please do."

Jonas stared at her and then took a deep breath. "Well," he continued, "you see, my wife has seen Dr. Jean Marc working on the unit. She knows you are a couple. But it seems that Dr. Jean Marc has not been a respectable man. She has seen him with a young nurse on her unit, in compromising situations."

"Compromising situations?" Hayden asked, swallowing the lump that had risen in her throat. She felt like she had been punched in the stomach.

"Well, kissing and touching. On a recent night shift, she saw them in a closed and unoccupied patient room. They did not know that she saw them coming out of the room. As well, she saw them go to a car in the parking lot together after shift. I am so sorry, Miss Hayden, but I did not want you to be the last to know."

"I appreciate it, Jonas. I really do."

Hayden wanted to vomit. For the rest of her shift, her mood fluctuated between rage, sorrow, and humiliation. The shift could not end soon enough. Monday morning, as she left the hospital after her night shift, she looked and saw Jean Marc's bronco in his usual spot.

Maybe Jonas is mistaken.

Regardless, she could barely focus on her drive home. When she got home and walked through the door, her emotions let go. She cried herself to sleep.

Hayden woke at 3:00 p.m. There were no texts from Jean Marc. She made herself toast and scrambled eggs and sat and stared at the TV. An hour went past, and she had no recollection of what she had even watched. At 8:00 p.m., she ordered in a pizza and ate two slices of it with three-quarters of a bottle of wine.

Tuesday morning, she woke hung-over and miserable. She checked her phone and was surprised to see a text from Jean Marc:

Want to have dinner tonight? I actually think I have a breather! Hope you are having a good day off! Love, JM xxoo

Hayden hopped in the shower and then got dressed. She was on a mission. On the drive, her heart pounded. Was she being irrational?

She turned left, and she could see Calgary Memorial Hospital ahead. She pulled into the staff parking lot, but Jean Marc's bronco was not in his usual spot.

What are you doing? Are you going to go up to the Unit and confront him?

She knew that this was not wise. She sat there contemplating. She pulled out her phone and texted him back.

That should work for dinner! Are you at the hospital now?

Jean Marc texted her back quickly:

Yes, of course, I'm here. Remember, this is my second home! ☺

She sighed and decided that she would talk to him at dinner tonight. Hayden pulled away and started to head towards the exit of the staff parking lot.

There were orange traffic pylons set up at the first exit, forcing her to drive to another exit farther down in the parking lot. That is when she saw Jean Marc's bronco, parked in a new spot. She steered her car towards it instead of the exit.

As she pulled up, she saw something familiar, a fluttering white note under his windshield wiper.

Don't do it.

Putting her car in park, she looked around and then got out. She walked over to his vehicle. The note had a red lipstick imprint on it. She yanked it out from the windshield wiper and opened it.

Hey, Handsome! Thank you for the cute note; now it is your turn! Can't wait to see you after my trip. I will be back on Friday. B xxoo

CHAPTER 19

Branta canadensis

Back in grade school, Hayden had researched and studied Canada geese. As part of her school curriculum, they had taken an exciting field trip into Calgary to the Inglewood Bird Sanctuary. It is situated off the Bow River, not far from Calgary Memorial Hospital. In her study, she learned that Canada geese mate for life and often refuse to leave the side of a sick or injured mate, even if winter is approaching and other geese in the group are flying south. This always stuck with Hayden. Honesty, monogamy, and loyalty were compulsory traits to her in a relationship, especially if there was any chance that it could lead to marriage.

Hayden drove home. She thought she would cry again, but all she could feel was numbness. She texted Jean Marc back that 5:00 p.m would work for dinner and asked if he could pick her up.

She couldn't focus on much that day; she mostly thought about what she was going to say. She had fluctuating moments of tears and then anger. By 4:00 p.m, she was mentally exhausted. She had a plastic bag at the door with any belongings of his that she had gathered. A few minutes before five, he knocked on the door.

"Hey!" he smiled and leaned forward and hugged her after she opened the door. Immediately, he knew something was amiss. "What's wrong?"

"Come in and sit down," Hayden said. She wanted to do this maturely.

If Jean Marc was nervous or guilty, there was no evidence of that on his face.

Hayden got right to the point. "Are you cheating on me Jean Marc?" She looked him right in the eyes.

"What are you talking about?" he scoffed.

"I asked you a question," she said quietly.

"Hayden, I am not having sex with anyone else. Where is this craziness coming from?"

"I asked you if you are cheating on me. Cheating isn't always just about sex, Jean Marc. Is there someone else?"

He swallowed but then laughed nervously. "You know me, I can be a flirt sometimes, but that is not cheating. My dad was the same. It is the French in us!"

"So, who was the note from on your windshield?" she asked, deadpan.

Jean Marc's eyes flashed with anger like a lightning bolt. "What, are you stalking me now, Hayden? What the fuck?" He got up from the couch.

"So, there is someone else," Hayden whispered flatly.

"It's nothing, Hayden, just harmless flirting. You are overreacting." Jean Marc's face was red.

Hayden walked to the door and picked up the bag, handing it to him. She was calm, but her eyes filled with tears. "Please leave."

"Hayden, come on! This is crazy; she is just a friend! You are being just like my mom when my dad had ladies he worked with. I am a doctor, and I work with lots of women. You are just overreacting!"

"How'd that work out for your parents, Jean Marc?" Hayden said coldly as she held the door open.

He stared at her and then took a deep breath. He took the bag from her hand and stepped out. He turned slightly as if he was going to say something else, but Hayden shut the door.

Hayden went and laid on her bed, expecting to cry, but she was out of tears.

The next day, she got up and showered and was determined to try to make the most of her days off. She was about to go to buy a tea when there was a knock at her door. She was relieved to see it was Lena.

"Hayden, I'm so sorry dear, did I wake you?" Lena was wringing her hands.

"No, no. I am up and around. Is everything okay, Lena?" Hayden said in concern.

"Well, I heard from my sister-in-law last night that my brother John had a heart attack. He lives in Edmonton, so my niece Candace is coming over, and I will go up with her to the hospital in Edmonton to see him. Would there be any chance you could look after Finnegan for the next two days?" she pleaded.

"Oh, I am so sorry to hear that, Lena. Of course, I can look after him!" She leaned over and hugged her.

"Can you pop up to my place? I will give you his leash, dishes and such." Lena shuffled up to her back door and went inside. Hayden waited at the back door.

Finnegan came running from inside the house, wagging his tail.

"Hi, my pup!" Hayden picked him up and cuddled him. Lena came to the back door, looking more distressed.

"Oh, Hayden, I am so sorry. Finn's kibble is almost empty. Here's twenty dollars, if you don't mind picking up some more. I am so sorry to inconvenience you. Here is a key to the house if you need anything."

"It's all good, Lena. Please have safe travels to Edmonton. You have my number if you need anything, and I hope all the best for your brother."

Hayden was grateful to have her furry friend keep her company. She changed her plans for the day and instead took Finnegan for a walk. It was sunny, but there was a cool wind. The leaves were falling more rapidly now.

Back at her place, she frequently checked her phone. She wasn't sure if she was disappointed or relieved that there was no communication from Jean Marc.

Thursday of her stretch of days off, she ended up raking leaves for Lena in the front and backyard, allowing Finnegan to romp in the grass and leaves. She called her mom and told her about Jean Marc. Her mom was comforting to her, but she sensed an undertone of relief that they had split up. Winnie later emailed her a poem about breakups and that 'kisses aren't contracts, and presents aren't promises.'

"Come home for Thanksgiving, Hayden, and we will have some nice family time," she had encouraged her on the phone.

Tomorrow was her last day off. She felt annoyed with herself that she didn't do anything fun, like getting together with friends. Both Ally and Clairese had texted her, asking her to get together but she had feigned illness. That night, she and Finnegan were on her couch watching a movie. Hayden had even made popcorn in an attempt to cheer herself up. Her phone buzzed, and she looked on the screen to see it was Shelby calling her. She decided to answer, and they spoke for over an hour. Shelby was supportive and listened to Hayden.

"Aren't you glad that you found out now and not later on in the relationship?" she posed.

Hayden was fast asleep, with Finnegan curled up next to her when her phone buzzed in the dark. Blurry-eyed, she looked at the screen. It was 2:05 a.m, and it was Jean Marc calling her.

"Hello?" she mumbled.

"Hayden, please don't hang up. I really miss you!" Jean Marc pleaded.

Hayden knew he was drunk. *This should be interesting.*

"Jean Marc you are drunk. Don't you have to work tomorrow?" she sighed into the phone.

"It's just a seminar tomorrow. It's not compulsory. Not to worry." He slurred his words. "Hayden, please, won't you give me a second chance? I miss you, and I really love you."

Her heart skipped a beat, and she squeezed her eyes closed tightly. Hot tears ran onto her pillow. "Jean Marc, why can you only say that to me when you are drunk?"

"That's not true. And you've never even said it to me, but I know in my heart that you love me, Hayden. I know you do." He whispered the last words. "I messed up, but it won't happen again, I promise."

Hayden sighed into the phone. "Can we talk about this tomorrow, or at least at a more reasonable hour?"

"I'm sorry, but I can't stop thinking of you. I know you have to work tomorrow, but yeah, we can talk later." Jean Marc agreed.

Hayden didn't correct him and say that she had the day off tomorrow. She thought she would leave the ball in his court and let him arrange their next meeting.

She heard him take a drink of whatever was his poison. "We were so good together, in EVERY aspect, if you know what I mean?" Jean Marc slurred again.

Hayden sat up, Finnegan looking at her quizzically, probably annoyed at being awoken.

"Jean Marc, I need to go back to sleep. You need to sleep this off, too. Let's talk later, okay?" Hayden lay back down.

"Okay, gorgeous. I love you. A bientot." Jean Marc's phone clicked off before she could reply. Hayden took a deep breath and closed her eyes. Her mind was racing, but she was able to fall back asleep.

Friday morning, she woke up late and with raging menstrual cramps and her period early. She felt bloated after her salty popcorn the night before. She got up and let Finnegan out to pee. She flopped back down on her bed. Did she dream that conversation last night, or did it really happen? She looked at her phone in her 'recents.' There it was, at 2:05 a.m.

She could hear Finnegan scratching at his dish. She got up and went into her kitchen.

"Oh, shit!" she exclaimed aloud, realizing she hadn't purchased his kibble as Lena had requested. She poured the few crumbs left in the bag into his dish and added a milk bone.

She looked in her fridge, which was also sparse. Her stomach growled, and Finnegan scratched the dish again.

"Okay, Buddy. I will be back shortly."

In the bathroom, she pulled her hair into a greasy ponytail. She examined her face and was alarmed at her acne breakout. *All stress-related,* she thought. Hayden pulled on her sweats and a baggy T-shirt. Comfort was the order of the day.

She drove over to the local supermarket, grabbed her cart, and began her shop. The produce was especially fresh today. She chose pomegranates, McIntosh apples, kiwis, and bananas for her fruit. She added spaghetti squash, peppers, and salad ingredients to her cart for her vegetable choices. She grabbed a fresh loaf of bread, yogurt, milk, and cheese. Not forgetting Finnegan, she went down the pet aisle and grabbed his kibble.

Hayden's stomach growled. *You shouldn't shop when you are hungry, and on your period,* she thought as she turned down the cracker and snack aisle. Standing there contemplating her choice, she heard female giggling and then a familiar male laugh. She looked up to see Jean Marc with a petite, blonde-haired woman hanging on his arm, approaching Hayden down the aisle. The woman was probably around twenty-two, appeared of maybe half-Asian descent, and with her hair obviously dyed blonde. She had fake eyelashes (which looked like caterpillars on her eyes), fake long nails, and she was wearing leggings and a tight yoga shirt. Jean Marc froze when he saw Hayden, and the girl stared at Hayden, blinking indifferently with those big, caterpillar lashes.

Hayden remembered the note on his windshield. *"Can't wait to see you after my trip; I will be back on Friday. B xxoo".* She remembered the lipstick on the note, too.

So, this must be "B," and Jean Marc thinks I am working today. I guess he skipped the seminar.

"Hi, Jean Marc," Hayden said flatly. She couldn't believe that she could even form the words. Her mouth was dry as a desert.

He swallowed. "Hi, Hayden. Uh, this is Brittany, and Brittany, this is Hayden."

"Oh, hey!" gushed Brittany. "You work in ICU, right? I saw you at a code on my unit once."

Hayden nodded and then smiled thinly. Obviously, Jean Marc had never told Brittany about Hayden. *Of course, this would happen when I look my worst.* Hayden thought grimly.

"Well, we should grab our stuff and get going. Just picking up snacks for the Seminar this afternoon on unit fifty-five," Jean Marc said quickly, moving away from Brittany's grip on his arm. He grabbed some potato chips, and Brittany grabbed cheese puffs and nacho chips.

"Nice to meet you!" Brittany chirped as they walked away. Jean Marc glanced back at Hayden; his face was drained of color, and he looked like he was going to be sick.

After they were gone, Hayden was left frozen, standing in the aisle, clutching her cart. She stared at the snacks blankly, unable to process a thought.

"Excuse me, ma'am," Hayden's thoughts were interrupted. She looked up to see a teenage boy trying to get at the snacks she was standing in front of.

"I'm sorry," she mumbled, moving out of the way. She looked at the empty end of the aisle, and then suddenly, rage rose in her throat. She pushed her cart to the end of the aisle and turned down the back aisle. She probably looked like a madwoman, pushing her cart quickly, scanning the end of each aisle for them as she drove. Then she saw them. They were standing in front of the deli and Brittany was hanging on his arm again, looking up to him adoringly. Jean Marc was staring straight ahead as the man behind the deli counter was handing them a large cheese and meat tray. They had obviously obtained a cart, which stood next to them. Brittany had let go of Jean Marc's arm and was accepting the tray from the deli man when Hayden reached them. She bumped her cart into theirs. Brittany jumped back with a startled look on her face. Jean Marc looked terrified.

"Don't you ever call me again at fucking two in the morning, professing your love for me. As a matter of fact, don't ever fucking call me again, Jean Marc," Hayden yelled.

People shopping nearby stopped what they were doing and were staring. The deli man's mouth hung open in shock. Brittany also looked terrified now.

Hayden turned her cart around. She needed deli meat too, but she didn't care. She drove her cart to a self-checkout. She was shaking, but she didn't regret what she had done.

As she paid for her purchases at the till, she looked up to see Brittany and Jean Marc leaving the store. Brittany gave her a dirty look, and Jean Marc mouthed, "I'm sorry," as they walked out. Hayden looked back at the terminal, trying to focus on her purchase.

As she pushed her cart out the door, a cashier near the exit cheerily called, "Have a good day!" Obviously, she was unaware of the scene at the deli. Hayden gripped her shopping cart tightly as she walked towards her car in the parking lot. She was confident that Jean Marc and Brittany were long gone. *What would that conversation sound like in the car*? She laughed aloud, humorlessly.

She loaded her purchases in the trunk and then pushed the cart back to the cart kiosk. Suddenly, she heard a familiar honking sound. She looked up to see a single Canada goose fly over. She looked for its mate, but there wasn't one.

Jean Marc was never my Branta canadensis, she thought as she got in her car.

CHAPTER 20

Downward Spiral

Hayden headed home, her veins still filled with adrenaline after the encounter with Jean Marc and Brittany. She fed Finnegan his kibble, and he gobbled it down. She thought some fresh air and a walk would do her good. She needed the distraction.

Despite the wind this week, there were still tons of leaves on the trees and the colors were vivid and spectacular. As she and Finnegan walked, she loved the sound of the crunch of the dried leaves under her shoes. She continued to admire the foliage in the adjacent river valley along the pathway but then stopped halfway and seated herself on a park bench. Finnegan sat down obediently next to her. Hayden enjoyed people-watching. She observed runners, moms pushing strollers, and some elderly people went past her along the path, also enjoying the sunshine. Hayden thought about the grove of aspen trees on the farm and how she used to build leaf forts with Paddy in the fall.

It wasn't long before her thoughts inevitably went back to Jean Marc. She sighed heavily and decided to begin their walk back home. She had promised herself to keep busy for the fall and aim to make more happy memories. It certainly was not going in that direction. She contemplated her return to work tomorrow; was she going to be able to keep it together? What happened if she ran into him in the hospital? She watched as a leaf spiraled down from a tree above to the ground. *Is that what my autumn is going to be, a downward spiral again*? She shook her head. Her break up with Jean Marc could never, ever compare to what she went through with Wyatt's death.

As she and Finnegan approached their community, she elected to walk down the street instead of cutting through the back alley. She loved the canopy of trees on the street and how everyone in this neighborhood took such pride in their yards. Hayden loved Halloween and Christmas when everyone decorated their yard.

"Did you enjoy our walk and fresh air, Finnegan?" Hayden asked as she unlocked the side gate. Entering the backyard, Hayden was alarmed to see the back door to Lena's house open. Although the screen door was closed, she knew someone must be in the house and would be surprised that Lena was back already. She pulled her phone out of her pocket and was contemplating whom to call when Finnegan started to bark, startling Hayden. She looked up to see Larry and Jezz coming out the back door.

"We wondered where the mutt was," Jezz laughed with a sour look on his face.

"What are you two doing?" Hayden asked, frowning and pulling Finnegan over to her. He continued to growl, which alarmed her.

"What business is that of yours? This is Larry's mom's house. You are just the renter in the basement," Jezz said scornfully.

Hayden ignored him. "Even if this is your mom's house, Larry, I don't think she would want you in there when she is not home."

"I know she is away, and I am just checking up on things for her," Larry said, folding his arms in front of him.

They stood in a bit of a standoff, and that is when Hayden noted the bruises on Larry's forearms. He must have noticed her staring at them, and he self-consciously slipped on the windbreaker he had tied around his waist.

"I have a key, Larry. I am looking after Finnegan, and she asked me to check on the house." Her last comment was a bit of a stretch, but she was confident that Lena did not ask Larry to check on the house.

Larry took a deep breath and then turned to Jezz. "Let's go." They walked past Hayden towards the garage in the back, Jezz giving her the death glare.

For a fleeting moment, she wondered if Larry had a key to his mom's place, did he also have a key to her suite? A chill ran down her spine.

Hayden locked Lena's door and returned to her own place. She decided to make some muffins and then later call her mom. That evening, she decided to text Clairese and Ally and tell them that she and Jean Marc broke up. It may save her from some awkward conversations at the hospital.

Very early the next morning, Hayden woke and lay staring at the ceiling, psyching herself up for the day. She took Finnegan for a dash around the block before she went to work, so she was a bit later than usual when she came into the break room for morning report. There was lots of chatter going on.

"What is happening?" she whispered to Ally.

"Management decided to make group changes. Everyone is switched around. It is effective come December 1st. I am kind of glad I am moving so I don't have to deal with that," she whispered back.

Hayden's heart sank. Group change happened every few years, and it always evoked lots of emotions. Your group was your family, you learned who you could count on, and you celebrated all events together. Hayden was already so sad that Ally was leaving; she dreaded to see if she was moved to a different group or who from her group might be leaving.

"Hayden, you better check out the list to see if your rotation changes, especially if you and Jean Marc are making travel plans," Danni suggested.

Hayden's felt her face flush. "We broke up, so that doesn't matter." she blurted out.

The room fell silent. Hayden looked over at Louise, who genuinely looked shocked. Jean Marc obviously had not told her.

The silence became awkward. "Okay, let's talk about group change later, everyone. Here is the assignment for tonight," Peggy said, attempting to change the subject.

After the assignment was read out, Hayden grabbed the group change sheet. She was assigned to stay in her group, but Shaye, Alana, and Jonas were moving to another group. With Ally leaving, too, Hayden felt like her allies were gone. That left Betty, Danni, Louise, and Kennedy, among others. She looked at who was joining her group: No-nonsense Nancy, Priya (who she liked), Gary (who worked at the pace of a sloth), and Kelda, who was loud and obnoxious. She and Louise would mix like oil and water. If Peggy left, it would be Carl (Snarl) and who knows for the other Clinician.

Keep it together, Hayden.

She got up and went into the ICU for her bedside report. After the report, she went in and started assessing her patient. Her patient was extubated and had an oxygen mask in place. Hayden was grateful she could actually converse with her patient to keep her focused. Her patient expressed feeling cold, so Hayden stepped out to obtain a warm blanket for her. Danni approached her in the equipment and supply room.

"Hayden, I am really sorry about my comment. I had no idea." She looked sincere.

"No problem. Thanks, Danni." She brushed past her, heading back to her patient's room.

When Peggy came by to check in, she sat down with Hayden at her workstation. Her pregnancy was visibly showing now.

"Hayden, management considered my recommendation for the group change. I wanted you to stay in this group in the hope that you will be considered for the clinician position. We really need strong leadership for this group coming up." She whispered the last sentence to Hayden.

Hayden nodded. "I appreciate that, Peggy." *Did she really*?

"I am sorry to hear about you and Jean Marc," she said, squeezing her hand. Hayden was grateful that with that brief but meaningful gesture, Peggy got up and went to the next bedside. She could feel the lump in her throat rising and needed to be alone.

Louise avoided her until Hayden headed into the medication room at about 9:30 a.m.

"Hayden, what happened with you and Jean Marc? I thought you made such a great couple! He really adores you."

Hayden stopped what she was doing and stared ahead briefly. It was none of her fucking business. Despite that, Hayden turned to her.

"He cheated on me, Louise." With that, she grabbed her IV medication and walked out of the room. By the genuinely shocked look on her face, Louise obviously knew nothing about Brittany either.

Coffee break time came. Ally came by her room. "Let's go sit outside for break Hayden," she suggested. It was a fabulous idea.

Nothing was said until they sat outside on the staff patio adjacent to the cafeteria. Yesterday, Hayden was scared at the thought of running into Jean Marc. Today, *he* should be the one scared to see *her.*

"I can't believe Danni!" Ally said, shaking her head. "She barely says anything any other time, and then today, she comes out with that!"

"I don't fault her," Hayden said, munching her homemade muffin.

Just then, Alana and Shaye joined them. "I hope you don't mind that I invited them," Ally questioned with a reassuring smile.

Alana and Shaye both hugged Hayden. "We're so sorry about Dr. Dumbhead, and we are going to miss you with group change!" they cried.

Hayden was grateful for this show of support from her colleagues and friends. The four of them sat for their break on the patio, the autumn sun on their backs. They laughed and joked, and it helped Hayden get through the rest of her shift.

At the end of her shift, she still instinctively looked for Jean Marc's red bronco in his parking spot, but there was a blue Toyota parked there now. She climbed into her car and put on her seatbelt. She had held it together all day, but she couldn't hold back anymore and started to cry. She had to get it out of her system.

She composed herself after a few minutes and then started her vehicle. A few leaves spiraled down from the tree in front of her vehicle, onto her windshield. She took a deep breath and drove home.

CHAPTER 21

Thanksgiving

The next few weeks for Hayden flew by. Each day, it seemed to get better. She looked forward to going home for Thanksgiving; she was grateful to have the weekend off work. She planned to go and visit Shelby, Dean, and the girls. Shelby's parents, Tate and June, were going to be spending the weekend with them, so Hayden looked forward to seeing them too.

At the end of September, Clairese invited Hayden out for lunch and a ride out to her favorite garden center, just outside the city limits. "I want to get some big pumpkins and some yellow and orange potted Mums for my doorstep!"

They had a wonderful lunch at a local shawarma and falafel place. Clairese shared that she and her policeman boyfriend Simon were getting quite serious and were considering moving in together.

"Well, at least he didn't check your height and weight on the police registry before your first date!" Hayden laughed, thinking back to her first date with Kevin. That seemed like a lifetime ago.

They arrived at the Honeybee's Country Garden Center and parked. In addition to plants and supplies for the garden, it also had a large home décor section. They were browsing through there together when Hayden felt someone touch her arm.

"Hayden Barrett, is that you?"

Hayden looked up and was surprised to see Imogene, Chunk's ex-girlfriend. She was wearing a smock, indicating that she was an employee at the garden center.

"Gena, it's been so long! How are you? I didn't know you lived in Calgary."

Hayden introduced Gena to Clairese, and they all chatted about what a great garden center it was.

"Yeah, I would love to run one of my own someday," Gena said wistfully. Then she looked at Hayden. "Have you seen Dylan when you have been at home?"

Hayden sighed. "Yeah, he is not doing well, Gena. I don't think he is working, and he is drinking a lot. I ran into him several weeks back."

Gena's eyes filled with tears. "That is what I have heard."

Hayden went out on a limb. "Why don't you go and see him, Gena? I am sure he would appreciate it."

Deep down, Hayden really wasn't that sure he *would* appreciate it, but she thought if there were anyone he might listen to, it would be Gena.

Gena nodded, then took a deep breath and smiled. "Let's go find you ladies some perfect pumpkins and potted Mums."

Later that afternoon, it was raining outside, and Hayden was curled up on her couch, reading a book. Her phone buzzed, and she picked it up to read a text from Bronwyn at Co-Op travel. Hayden exhaled deeply. Jean Marc or Louise had never paid her, but Bernie had sent her his $250.00. He had e-transferred her the money after she and Jean Marc broke up, with a message saying: "I am sorry it took so long to send this. I am sorry about you and Jean Marc as well."

She texted Bronwyn, saying she would drop by on Thanksgiving Friday when she came into town. Hayden wasn't sure what she was going to do; she fully anticipated she could lose the remaining $500.00 she was out of pocket for the trip for four that was never going to happen. *Maybe Louise, Bernie, Jean Marc, and Brittany could all go instead,* she thought cynically.

Hayden had traded some shifts with some other nurses on the unit to have a four-day stretch off for Thanksgiving. She planned to leave Thursday afternoon after she had slept part of the day since she was working Wednesday night.

On Monday and Tuesday, she noticed that Lena had not raked leaves in the yard much. However, they seemed to be falling faster than you could rake them. Hayden had packed her belongings and had some time before she went to work, so did some raking herself. She was putting the rake back in the garage when she saw Lena at the back door.

"Hayden, thank you so much! I haven't been feeling up to doing much lately." Lena looked profoundly sad again.

"Are you ill, Lena?" Hayden asked, concerned.

"No, I just am feeling blue. It sometimes happens to me at this time of year."

Tell me about it. Hayden thought. She had told bits and pieces about Wyatt to Lena, but she did not know the whole story.

"Well, I hope you have a nice Thanksgiving, Lena," Hayden said and hugged her.

"Well, I am going to my niece Candace's for dinner. You have a nice Thanksgiving too, Hayden. Say hello to your family."

The next morning, when Hayden came home from her night shift, there was an envelope with her name on it, taped to her door. When she opened it and read the letter inside, her heart sank.

She immediately went and knocked on Lena's door. There was no answer, but she could hear Finnegan barking. She tried calling Lena on her phone, but it just rang. She reread the letter.

> *Dear Hayden Barrett:*
>
> *I have been increasingly concerned about my mother's wellbeing, especially with winter approaching. With that in mind, she has agreed to relocate to an Assisted Living facility. I will be moving into her home and upkeeping it in her absence. I also plan to complete some long-needed renovations and repairs. Regretfully, I must inform you that I am giving you notice to vacate your accommodation in the basement by December 1st. This letter is effective for November 1st, giving you more than thirty days' notice to leave the premises.*
>
> *Thank you for your prompt attention to this.*
>
> *Larry Rickleson*

Hayden couldn't sleep after her nightshift, with this letter on her mind. Poor Lena! She loved her garden, and what would happen to Finnegan? She knew some senior facilities did allow dogs, so she hoped for that. Was Larry's concern really sincere? What possible renovations needed to be done here? Lena's place was immaculate and so well kept.

Selfishly, she also thought, where am I going to go? The vacancy rate in the city was not that great. She loved her location here, the neighborhood, and all the nearby amenities.

By noon, she had only slept fitfully, so she gathered her belongings, made herself a strong travel mug of tea, and headed to her vehicle. She knocked on Lena's door once more before leaving, but there was still no answer.

She was never so glad to be pulling into the yard of her farm. Butch ambled over to give her his usual greeting. Hayden didn't even unload her things from the car; she just headed inside. Her mom met her at the door, and Hayden was already crying.

They spent the afternoon talking about Lena and possible places that Hayden could live. Hayden also lamented about moving in the winter. The scenario just kept getting worse. When Paddy and her dad came in from the field, she was more composed, and she shared her situation with them. Her eyes welled with tears, though, when Paddy hugged her saying, "It will be all right, Sister."

Hayden drove into town by herself the next day. Her parents or Paddy never questioned it, but she did not want to tell them about her cancelled trip or the thousand-dollar deposit she may be losing.

Bronwyn never pressed her when she said her 'circumstances had changed.' It was probably apparent by reading Hayden's face.

"I can pull some strings, Hayden, and see if I can extend the travel period to another time and even another destination. However, the 'group of four' situation kind of sticks, unfortunately. Have you considered a possible trip with your family?" she proposed.

"I really appreciate anything you can do, Bronwyn. I don't think the family trip would work; my dad can't and probably won't leave the cattle for that long."

Bronwyn nodded in understanding. "I can hold it for another six months, max. Just get back to me when you can."

Hayden thanked her and left her office. She walked over to *Blainey's Bakery* to buy some of Paddy's favorite cheese rolls. After that, she headed over to the *Crow and Crocus* to buy her mom a festive little pepper plant. Her last stop was at the liquor store for a six-pack of her dad's favorite beer. He didn't drink often, so this would be a treat.

It was two in the afternoon, and the sun was hot. Southern Alberta was enjoying an 'Indian Summer' of heat for the Thanksgiving weekend. She sat in her car for a moment, with her window rolled down, hesitating. She took a deep breath, then got back out and walked back to the *Crow and Crocus.* At the store entrance, she had seen they had beautiful autumn arrangements of sunflowers, orange Gerbera daisies, red chrysanthemums, and sprigs of wheat. Hayden purchased an arrangement and went back to her car. Instead of heading back to the farm, she turned her car back towards the entrance into town.

She pulled down the side gravel road and parked on the grassy shoulder, next to a grove of aspen trees. There was no one around, so she had the cemetery to herself. She left the window down on her car since it was so warm. Walking over to the black wrought iron gate, it squeaked when she opened it. As she walked past all the stones, she surprisingly felt completely at peace. A crow cawed as he flew over, and she could hear some songbirds chirping back in the grove of trees. Hayden could see the familiar stone ahead with the large inscription: 'Montgomery' displayed across the top. Some flowers were lying on the grass in front of it; someone had obviously been here in the last few days. As she approached closer, she saw a bottle of beer next to the stone. It was Wyatt's favorite brand. Hayden smiled and shook her head: *Chunk*, she chuckled.

She sat down in the crunchy leaves and soft grass and faced Wyatt's gravestone. *Forever cherished, Forever loved*, it read. She laid her flower arrangement in front of her.

"*I am sorry it's been so long since I've been here.*" she quietly said aloud.

Hayden didn't say much more but instead sat there and reminisced about all their time together. The sun was warm and comforting on her back, and an occasional warm breeze gently lifted the hair at her temples. She heard a car approaching behind her, and she looked down at her watch. She was surprised that a whole hour had passed. She kissed her hand and then touched Wyatt's stone.

Hayden walked back to her vehicle. She vaguely knew the elderly couple that was approaching the cemetery, and she nodded politely. Getting back into her car, she was glad she had come. All this time, Hayden had thought coming here again would give her more pain, but instead, it offered her great comfort.

She turned her car around slowly on the narrow road so that she could head back to town. At that moment, another car was turning off the highway to come into the cemetery. She was glad that she had the solitude there when she did. Nodding politely as the vehicle passed, she recognized the man driving as a recent widow from town.

Stopping at the secondary highway, she had to wait for traffic both ways before she could turn left. Hayden was initially surprised at all the traffic but then recalled it was Thanksgiving weekend, so many visitors may be coming and going. As she waited, the breeze from her open window again gently tousled her hair. Suddenly, she felt a tickle on the right side of her neck. She flicked her hand quickly, afraid it was a spider crawling on her. Looking down as it landed in her lap, she gasped. It was a ladybug.

She stared at it and then smiled. *I know you are watching over me, Wyatt.*

CHAPTER 22

Lena

The rest of the Thanksgiving weekend was lovely. On Sunday, Hayden went out to visit Shelby and Dean, and the girls. June and Tate were there and were so happy to see Hayden. Maybe it was her visit to the cemetery, but Hayden felt completely at ease with them all. They even reminisced over stories of Wyatt during the visit. When Hayden was leaving, June hugged her and whispered in her ear, "Wyatt loved you so much Hayden. We want you to be happy, and we hope you can find someone to do that with."

Thanksgiving dinner at home on Sunday was delicious and an enjoyable event. Hayden and Winnie cooked all afternoon, resulting in a wonderful feast. Ced's sister and brother-in-law, Sylvia and Willus Clancy, joined them for dinner. Hayden's uncle Willus owned and ran the hardware store in town. During dinner, Ced shared a surprising piece of news with Hayden.

"I ran into an old friend of yours at Uncle Willus' store last week, Hayden."

"Oh, who was that, Dad?" Hayden asked curiously.

"It was Dylan or Chunk as you kids all used to call him. He was there getting some parts for work." Ced smiled.

"He is back working with his dad and seems to have cleaned his act up," Willus added, nodding approvingly.

Hayden smiled. "I am so glad to hear that." She wondered if Gena had been in touch with him or if Chunk had done this on his own accord. She knew that if he had done this on his own initiative, that he would potentially have better success.

Thanksgiving Monday, she spent on the farm helping her mom clean up the garden and flowerbeds in preparation for the winter. It was still warm today, but there was a cool breeze, hinting at what was to come. Ced was over at a neighboring farm, helping with the last of their harvest. Paddy had even gone to help as well.

Winnie made an early supper and packed up tons of leftovers for Hayden to take back home. As Hayden neared the city limits in her car, her thoughts turned back to her breakup with Jean Marc, her impending group change at work, but most of all, where she was going to find a place to live. All the sadness she had set aside this past weekend came bubbling back up in her throat. "Why worry about something you have no control over?" Ced had reinforced. Winnie had encouraged her to "Take one day at a time." Hayden decided that on her next days off, she would start looking for a place to move to. If she could find a place soon, she could move before the snow flies. Then she thought of Lena and Finnegan, and sadness washed over her all over again.

As she turned into her alley, she was alarmed to see a police car parked near Lena's garage. An ambulance was just leaving and pulling out the other end of the alley, with its emergency lights on. When it pulled onto the street, the sirens turned on.

What the hell is going on? She pulled up, not even going into the garage, and jumped out of her car. A police officer in the backyard stopped her.

"Can I help you?" he asked, with his hand up.

"I live here, in the basement," Hayden said breathlessly. "What is going on?"

"Do you have any identification, Miss?"

"Yes, yes, it is in my car. Can you please tell me what is going on?"

"Apparently, the lady that lives here was found at the bottom of the basement stairs; she had fallen. She was just taken to the trauma center."

Hayden's eye's welled with tears. "How did this happen?"

"My partner is inside interviewing a family member. I guess I could permit you to go in." The police officer radioed to his partner.

As Hayden entered the back door, she could hear Finnegan barking in the distance. She walked into the living room. Another police officer was talking with Larry. Larry appeared disheveled. Hayden stared at Larry. "Where is Finnegan?" she asked flatly.

"He wouldn't stop barking. I put him in Mom's bedroom," he said with his hand on his forehead.

Hayden turned and went down the hall and opened the door. Finnegan almost leapt in her arms and licked her face. She went back to the living room, holding Finnegan.

The police officer asked her, "I understand you live in the basement? When did you see Mrs. Rickleson last?"

"I just drove here from my hometown. I have been away for four days. I had not seen Lena for a couple of days before that."

"Mom was at my cousin's for dinner on Sunday. I tried calling her several times today, and I couldn't reach her. I came over here tonight and found her at the bottom of the stairs, just outside the entrance to your place," Larry explained.

Hayden looked directly at the officer. "She probably was coming to talk to me. Larry here has elected to move Lena to a senior's facility, probably against her will, and he has also asked me to move out."

Larry whipped his head around. "What are you suggesting?" he sputtered. "I only have her best interests in mind."

Hayden refused to look at him. "And where is your sidekick, Jezz?"

The officer intervened. "Okay, Miss. I would like to finish speaking with Mr. Rickleson here. Could we come and speak to you later, or my partner could also talk to you as well."

"Fine," Hayden said and left Lena's house. She took Finnegan down to her place and saw blood on the laminate floor, as well as discarded medical wrappings from EMS having been there. Her throat hitched, and her eyes welled with tears.

Hayden put out some food and water for Finnegan. He curled up on her couch, probably exhausted from barking. She went back upstairs to the backyard. By this time, the sun was setting, and there was an orange glow in the sky.

She approached the officer. "I am happy to answer any questions for you, but I would really like to go and see Lena right now. Would you be able to tell me what hospital she was transferred to?"

He told her she had been taken to Calgary Memorial. The officer took down her cell phone number, and Hayden jumped back in her car and headed to the hospital emergency department.

When she got to triage, the nurse phoned into the department to check and see if Hayden could come back to visit. She hung up the phone and told Hayden that Lena was in radiology having a CAT scan. Hayden then asked if Clairese was on duty tonight. The triage nurse excused herself to check and returned with Clairese.

"Coyote, what are you doing here?" Clairese said in concern.

Hayden burst into tears and told her the story.

"That is poor Lena in the trauma bay? I had no idea, Hayden!" she said, embracing her. "Let's go over there. I think they were just bringing her back from CT."

The curtains to the first trauma bay were closed, so Hayden stood outside as Clairese went in to check. After a moment, Clairese emerged and beckoned Hayden in. "This is Mataya Reimer, our trauma surgeon today. Mataya, this is Hayden Barrett. She is an ICU nurse upstairs, and she lives with Lena."

"Hi, Hayden. I do recognize you. Does Lena have family?"

"She is widowed, but she has a son, Larry. He is back at the house being interviewed by the police because he is the one who found her at the bottom of the stairs," Hayden answered.

"Is foul play suspected? I never heard that with EMS' report," Mataya questioned.

Hayden saw Jezz's face flash before her. *Where was he*? Hayden shrugged.

Mataya looked concerned but then softened. "I understand from Clairese that Lena is very dear to you. I am sorry to tell you, Hayden, but her prognosis does not look good. She has a massive intracerebral bleed on her CT. I can show it to you on the PACS screen here."

As they all looked on the medical imaging screen, Hayden asked, "Is this a result of her falling down the stairs, or could it have happened and then she fell down the stairs as a result of it?"

"I believe that this happened before she fell. The rest of her injuries are consistent with that."

Maybe she was coming to see me because she felt ill, Hayden thought but knew it would not have made a difference in her prognosis.

Hayden thanked Mataya for her honesty and then asked to see Lena. She wanted to see her before Larry arrived.

Clairese held her hand as they entered the trauma bay. Staff in the room respectfully nodded and lowered their voices. Lena lay on the stretcher with the endotracheal tube in her mouth, her chest rising and falling with the ventilator's breaths.

"It is so much different seeing someone you know like this, instead of just your patient," Hayden whispered to Clairese, who nodded in agreement.

Hayden knew that this might be the last time she may see Lena alive, so she whispered some words of thanks and love to her in her ear. She sat and held her hand until the nurse looking after Lena told her that Larry was in the waiting room and wanted to come in to see her. Hayden wiped her tears and put her hand over the top of Lena's heart, leaned forward, and whispered in her ear, "Thank you for being my home away from home, Lena. I love you."

CHAPTER 23

End of October

Larry phoned her cell the following morning to tell her his mom had passed away. She had let it go to voicemail and listened after.

Hayden called in sick for her next two shifts. Word had gotten around, and she was receiving lots of texts from Ally, Alana, and Shaye. Clairese called her, saying that there was something waiting for her at her back door. Hayden opened her door to find a small pot of chili, two buns, and an apple crisp, all homemade. Her mom offered to come up to Calgary, but Hayden declined; she said she needed to work through this on her own.

Finnegan must have sensed something, as he stuck close to Hayden for those few days. When she let him out to pee, he didn't even go towards Lena's door.

The next day, there was a note taped to her door again. It was from Larry informing her of the plans for Lena's service. He also asked if she would consider taking Finnegan; otherwise, he would make 'other' arrangements. *What the fuck does that mean*?

There was no question of whether she would take Finnegan; she would have fought for him regardless.

The following Monday, there was a service for Lena at the church in the neighborhood. Not surprisingly, the church was packed with neighbors who loved Lena. Hayden was happy that Lena had a nice service to celebrate her life. Everyone knew of Lena's famous garden, so there was no shortage of flowers at the church, including the arrangement that Hayden had ordered. She knew that many florists in the city could have made it, but she ordered it from the *Crow and Crocus* in Willow Creek. Her mom drove up to support her for the funeral and brought the arrangement with her.

Larry was, of course, at the funeral, but Hayden did not go and speak with him. She just couldn't bring herself to do it. Jezz was nowhere to be seen at the funeral, but Hayden knew he was still lurking around. She had seen his car on the street in the last few days.

Back at the hospital, Hayden threw herself back into her work. It was now nearing the end of October; the days were colder, and snow was even forecasted to arrive soon. She tried to keep her mood upbeat. Halloween was nearing, usually an event that Hayden loved to decorate for, but she didn't even pull her decorations out of their boxes. Last year, she and Lena had handed candy out to the neighborhood kids together. She sighed heavily at the memory.

On her next day shift, Hayden slipped over to her manager's office on her coffee break.

"I have decided not to apply for Peggy's clinician job," she told her manager, Joan. "It is not a good time in my life for it right now."

"I am disappointed to hear that, Hayden, but I totally understand." Joan had nodded. "I hope you will reconsider it in the future when another opportunity arises."

Louise continued to be cordial to Hayden at work but was certainly more distant. She couldn't possibly be upset that Hayden did not attend her bridal shower; it had occurred on the day of Lena's funeral. Today, Hayden had noted a poster on the staff communication board that Louise, Bernie, and Jean Marc were hosting a Halloween party at their house and that everyone was invited. "Don't forget to dress up!" it said at the bottom of the poster. There was no mention of Brittany on the invite. *I guess she hasn't moved in yet*, Hayden thought cynically.

Once per year, staff in the ICU and CCU must complete their recertifications in skills. There is also a take-home exam they must complete. Staff is divided into spring or fall recertifications, and Hayden was fall. *Just one more thing on my plate to deal with,* she thought. On her morning break, Hayden looked in the staff mail file for her exam to complete. She was surprised to find an addressed envelope in her file with familiar handwriting on it. Opening it, she discovered a sympathy card from Jean Marc.

I know Lena was very special to you. Thinking of you at this time, JM

Her heart softened a bit, but it was still painful to think about him. She still had never run into him in the halls at the hospital, which she was grateful for. She no longer looked for his vehicle in the parking lot. Lena's death, her 'eviction' from her suite, and the group change were enough stressful things going on in Hayden's life. However, they had all been distractions for her from thinking of Jean Marc's and her unpleasant breakup.

Halloween came and went; Hayden ended up picking up a night shift for overtime that night. It gave some of her colleagues that had children the opportunity to go trick or treating with them. A few days after the Halloween party, Hayden overheard Kennedy talking about the 'fantastic' time they had over at Jean Marc and Bernie's place; she chose to ignore the conversation.

Hayden's days off work involved looking for a place to live, especially since Calgary already had received their first snowfall of the season on November 3rd. Now, she couldn't wait to get out of her place. Larry and Jezz had moved in and were (not surprisingly) terrible 'neighbors.' They argued frequently and were very loud; they never shoveled the walks, and one (or both of them) smoked weed, as the skunky smell wafted through the ventilation down to her place. They also told her (via another note on her door) that she had to park on the street so that they could both park their vehicles in the garage.

Finding a place that permitted dogs proved to be challenging and more expensive. Hayden would make an appointment at an apartment complex or townhouse, and it would either be a complete dump, 'pet friendly' would mean you could have a gerbil or a fish, or it was astronomically expensive. Hayden did not yet have the money to purchase her own place, and not having Finnegan was non-negotiable.

As November progressed, she became more panicky as to what she was going to do. Hayden needed to get out of this house; she felt like she had hit rock bottom. She didn't think she could face anything else adverse in her life. But she was wrong.

CHAPTER 24

Out of Left Field

The minute the Halloween decorations were away, Christmas season began. Hayden always found this distasteful to the Veterans and thought that the retail market should wait until at least after November 11th.

It was Hayden's turn to work Christmas this year, and secretly, she was almost glad. She knew she would still celebrate with her family at some point, but she was not in the mood for all the other festivities. All she could focus on right now was finding a place to live.

Her dad called her up in the middle of November. "I have a suggestion or temporary solution for you," he began. "Why don't you move all your furniture down here? We can store it in the Quonset. You can have Finnegan stay here. Maybe you can stay with one of your friends for the time being. We just gotta get you outta there, Bunny."

That sounded like a solution, at least temporarily. Hayden spent the next two days off packing, as her dad, mom, and Paddy would be here this weekend to help move her out. Who could she ask to let her stay on the upcoming days that she was scheduled to work?

Ally had moved to Edmonton already. They had a going-away supper for her one evening just before Halloween at a Greek restaurant. She knew who her next consideration would be. Hayden met with Clairese and posed the temporary arrangement to her. Clairese was thrilled with the idea. "We both work shifts, and I can stay over at Simon's, too. I am sure it will work, and I am happy to help you out!"

"It won't be for a long time, and I will pay you some rent money," Hayden promised.

As she was leaving Clairese's place, Simon was just pulling up in his car after a shift. He was still in uniform. It was nice to meet him finally, and he and Clairese looked so genuinely happy together.

Hayden got back to her place and did some last-minute packing and cleaning. She worked the next night and then was off for the weekend for her move. It was already the last week of November.

Her phone buzzed, and she saw it was Shelby. "Hey, Shelb," she answered.

"Hi, girl. I am just checking in to see how you are doing?" Shelby whispered.

"I am okay. How are you? Why are you whispering?"

"Hadley has been teething and screams every time I put her down. She is sleeping on my chest right now." Shelby sighed.

"Oh, poor you," Hayden chuckled.

"I understand you are coming home this weekend. I ran into your mom at the post office. Dean and I were hoping you could come to our place on Saturday night for a little pre-Christmas party. Mom and Dad are going to take the girls for the night."

"Please tell me you are not setting me up with someone," Hayden said suspiciously.

"No, nothing like that. However, there will be someone here that you might be surprised to see." Shelby continued to whisper.

"Who is that?" Hayden asked curiously.

"Chunk, I mean Dylan as he likes to be called now."

Hayden then told Shelby about her summer encounter with him and then her dad's story at Thanksgiving.

"He really struggled after Wyatt. Our family doesn't blame him. He is trying hard to get back on track," Shelby agreed. "And...he and Gena got back together this week. He asked if he could bring her."

Hayden said she would do her best to make an appearance. Then, as she lay in bed that night, contemplating it all, she thought she would just feel like a fifth wheel at the party with all the couples.

She awoke the next morning to Finnegan licking the tears on her face. She tried to remember what she was dreaming about before she woke. All she could recall was Wyatt and Chunk were there, and it was raining. Then she looked out her window and saw it was sleeting outside.

After a quick bite to eat, she took Finnegan on a quick run around the block. As she came in the back gate, she was startled to see someone at her back door.

"Hello?" she called out.

A woman in a grey jacket with the hood up turned around, startled. "Oh, Hayden, is that you?"

"Yes," Hayden replied, guarded.

"Oh, it's me, Candace Stratton. I am Lena's niece."

Relief washed over Hayden. "Oh, hi, Candace! Let's go into my place before we are both soaked!"

They went inside, and Candace surveyed the boxes sadly. "Aunt Lena told me at Thanksgiving that Larry had asked you to move out. I am sorry about that. I know you loved living here."

"Thank you, Candace. I will miss it, but it would never be the same without Lena here. And Larry is not the best neighbor." She didn't care if he was her cousin; she called him out.

Hayden was drying Finnegan off. Candace stared at him. "It gives me such peace that you are going to take custody of Finn. Lena loved that dog." Candace sighed. "She loved you too, Hayden, just like a granddaughter."

Hayden's eyes filled with tears.

"That is why I am here, Hayden. I have something for you." Candace pulled out a little jewel box with a ring in it. Hayden recognized Lena's engagement ring. Candace handed it to her. "I know she would have wanted you to have it."

"No, Candace, you are her niece! You should inherit it!" Hayden said incredulously. "Does Larry know you have it?"

"I don't give a shit," she scoffed. "He is stoned half the time now with that creep he lives with. He does not take any value or sentimentality in these things. The funeral home gave it to me, and he was right there when they did. He didn't seem to care."

Candace looked down at the ring in her hand.

"Aunt Lena told me that you had a special love one time that you lost." Her voice softened. "I hope you don't mind that she told me that."

Hayden shook her head. A tear rolled down her cheek.

"Anyway, she told me that she hoped and prayed that someday you would find true love as she did with Uncle Henry. This ring symbolizes that love. I already have my true love Hayden, and I think you should have this."

Hayden accepted the ring from Candace. It was a vintage triple diamond ring set in yellow gold. Hayden remembered Lena wearing it; she never wore it when she was gardening or baking.

"I am so glad that I caught you before you moved; it would have been challenging to track you down! I won't keep you any longer, Hayden." Candace moved towards the door.

Before she left, Candace hugged her. When she stepped back, she took both Hayden's hands in hers and smiled sincerely through her tears. "I hope you can find peace and true love again."

The next morning, Hayden sat in the report room waiting for the assignments to be read out by Peggy and Carl for ICU and CCU. People were chatting about Christmas parties and events they had coming up. Louise was prattling on about how Bernie's parents were hosting an upcoming *prestigious* dinner party and that she was looking forward to meeting so many people as 'the future daughter in law.'

Hayden's heart dropped a bit. She sadly thought of Wyatt, then Candace's words from last night echoed in her ears.

I hope you can find true love again.

Everyone made their way into the ICU or CCU for their shift. Hayden's patient was going to the OR imminently, so she completed a quick but thorough assessment on him. She looked over the OR check sheet, and soon, the call came to send him to the OR. Hayden saw him off and then went to her colleagues' assigned rooms to see if they needed her assistance with their patient care. Everyone was functioning well on their own, so she sat at her workstation and began working on completing her recertification exam.

She looked up from her exam to see two police officers enter the unit. It was not unusual to see police; sometimes, they obtained statements from family whose loved one was in ICU. They may have been involved in an accident, and the police may require more information in their investigation.

The police officers were speaking quietly to the unit clerk, Gurpreet. Gurpreet shook her head and then turned and asked Hayden, "Do you know where Peggy is?"

Hayden stood up. "I don't, but I can find her." Hayden popped her head in a few rooms and located her in Alana's patient's room.

Peggy proceeded to speak to the officers, and Hayden saw Peggy's face pale. She glanced over at Hayden, then turned back and ushered the police officers out of the unit.

Hayden felt her stomach drop. Alana came over and asked what was going on.

"I don't know," she said softly.

Peggy returned into the unit and approached Louise, who was just coming out of the medication room. "Can I speak to you outside for a moment, Louise?" Hayden could barely hear her from a distance down the unit.

Louise looked confused. Peggy led her out of the unit with her hand on her back. Suddenly, Hayden knew where they were going. There was a 'Family Quiet Room' outside the unit, where family conferences took place. It was a private place to talk.

"I somehow don't think this is going to end well," Hayden said apprehensively to Alana.

She had no sooner spoken than a blood-curdling scream came from the hall. Alana looked at Hayden in shock. Staff stepped out of their patient's room inquisitively with concerned looks on their faces.

The wail repeated and then, "NO, NO, NO!"

Peggy came back into the unit and beckoned Hayden over. Hayden jumped out of her chair, that familiar sick feeling rising in her throat. Peggy led Hayden out into the hall.

"They found Bernie at home...he has taken his own life. Can you take Louise to her house?"

"Of course," Hayden nodded apprehensively.

Just then, Kennedy came out of the CCU. "What happened to Louise?"

Hayden and Peggy looked at each other, both reluctant to share the news. Just then, the door of the Quiet Room flew open. "I need to go to him!" Louise screamed.

Coming out of the room, she looked at Hayden and then Kennedy. Then she turned her back on them. Facing one of the police officers, she sobbed into his chest, "Please take me to him now."

CHAPTER 25

Beginning of December

The 'group change' party, planned for the last day of November, was scaled back to a small potluck at one of the nurses' homes. The mood in the unit had changed to somber, out of respect for Louise. As well, group change always felt like a sad separation of family and friends, and no one was really in the celebration mood.

The story came out that Bernie had told Louise and Jean Marc that morning that he was sick, so they went to work without him. Later that morning, Bernie sent Jean Marc a cryptic text, so Jean Marc asked to leave to go back and check on him. He went home and found Bernie dead. Bernie did not leave a note for anyone, which left so many unanswered questions and anguish for those that loved and cared for him.

That day, Hayden stayed and completed her shift but did try and phone Jean Marc; it went straight to his voicemail. She left him a message, saying she was so sorry for his loss. Hayden also texted Louise a similar message and offered that if she needed anything, that she was more than willing to help her. As well, she sent them both sympathy cards in the mail. She never heard back from either of them.

Hayden found it difficult to make those calls to Jean Marc and Louise and say the right thing, even though she had experienced a traumatic death of a loved one herself. Even when she wrote out the cards, she struggled with the right words.

She reflected back to when Wyatt died and how some people said the most inappropriate things to her: "*I know how you must feel*" or "*It was such a tragedy, but you are young and will be able to move on.*" She remembered wanting to scream at those people, "*You have NO FUCKING IDEA how I feel*!" Or "*Your comment is SO inappropriate!"* Sometimes, people that she had known all her life said nothing at all to her and just appeared utterly uncomfortable. At the time, she thought people were so crass and uncaring. But, after witnessing so many tragic circumstances as a nurse, she realized that often, people mean well, and they truly don't know the proper thing to say. Or, they are so uncomfortable that they say nothing at all. She decided that she had done her best to send her condolences to them both.

Hayden, with the help of her family, moved all her furniture and belongings to the farm that weekend. She didn't really like living in limbo, but she wanted the Christmas season out of the way, and then she could have a fresh start for the New Year. She didn't want to inconvenience Clairese any longer than she had to. Clairese had a cat named Buzz, so having Finnegan there would not be a good idea. Hayden was confident that Paddy would give Finnegan lots of extra love back on the farm as an 'inside dog' until she could find a place for both of them to live. She felt bad for Finnegan; his world had been turned upside down in the last month.

Bernie's funeral was held the Friday of the first week of December. The church was packed. Ally came back down from Edmonton, and she, Hayden, Shaye, and Alana went together. They had anticipated Louise would be crying through most of the service, but she was stoic and/or in a state of shock. *Maybe she is sedated*, Ally had said. She was dressed all in black, with a hat and a veil, like Jackie Kennedy. Hayden sympathized with her but thought the veil was a bit over the top.

At the reception after the funeral, Hayden wanted to go over and speak to Jean Marc, but Brittany was glued to his arm the whole time.

"Just go and talk to him and ignore her!" Shaye had encouraged.

"He is the one that cheated, so *she* is the one that should be uncomfortable, not you!" Alana agreed with Shaye.

Hayden felt terrible, but she just couldn't get the courage to do it. However, they all went together and expressed their condolences to Louise, and each hugged her. Hayden thought Ally might have been right; Louise could barely mumble a word back to any of them.

Group change had happened, and Hayden missed her work friends that left the group. Louise was off on bereavement and then stress leave. Kennedy was back to work, but she ignored Hayden. Hayden decided to focus on work, and perhaps in January, she would plan a trip or something similar so that she would have something to look forward to. She was glad that she had never applied for the clinician position; although that would have been good experience, she certainly didn't need the extra stress in her life right now.

It was already the second week of December. Hayden had finished her Christmas shopping, as she knew she had many shifts ahead of her. Tonight was her first night shift of three. Going in for a night shift on a cold winter night was always so much harder than when the weather was pleasant.

Peggy was working her last few shifts before going off on maternity leave. It had not been announced who would be replacing her yet. After hearing her assignment, Hayden headed to the ICU for the bedside report. She was pleased to see Scarlett sitting there.

"Hey stranger!" Hayden greeted. "How was your shift?"

"It was super busy; this lady is really sick. You'll have your work cut out for you tonight!" Scarlett warned. "Hey, I am so sorry to hear about Bernie. I know he was a friend of yours. Hudson and I were in Saskatchewan visiting his parents, so we missed the service."

"Oh, thanks, Scarlett. Yeah, it was really sad," Hayden nodded.

Scarlett squeezed Hayden's hand.

"So, the story on your patient, Coraleigh McCabe, is she is sixty-two years old and postop from a cholecystectomy but now has developed sepsis. She is on CRRT for her kidney failure." Scarlett began. Over the next ten minutes, Scarlett gave a comprehensive head-to-toe report on Coraleigh.

"Her daughter, Ainsley, is at the bedside and is very attentive and super nice," Scarlett continued. "Her son is flying in here from Vancouver tonight. Her condition was quite unstable this afternoon, so they were very worried."

Sometimes it was difficult to have family members at the bedside continuously. It was like having another patient, especially if they questioned everything you were doing. Despite that, Hayden jumped right in, introduced herself to Ainsley, and started assessing Coraleigh. She did explain everything she was doing as she worked. Once she finished, she obtained assistance from colleagues to turn Coraleigh and settled her.

Ainsley looked exhausted. Hayden offered her a cup of tea and a warm blanket.

"Oh, that would be lovely!" she said gratefully, "I have hardly left Mom's bedside all day; I was too afraid to. My brother should be here soon, and then we are going to switch places. I have to get home to my hubby, kids, and two dogs!"

After Hayden got the tea and blanket, she pulled her 'computer on wheels' into the room as she completed her documentation. She could keep a closer eye on the continuous dialysis as well. Hayden also sensed that Ainsley could use the emotional support and company.

As the evening progressed, they chatted as Hayden gave care. She learned about Coraleigh's life: she was a widow and Ainsley, and her brother were her only children. Ainsley was married to Kip, and they had Coraleigh's only grandchildren, Emery and Callen. Their uncommon names led to a discussion of the origin of names.

"What is the significance of your name, Hayden?" Ainsley asked.

"It was my mom's maiden name. My parents were going to name me Hayden whether I was a boy or girl." Hayden smiled.

"Oh, that's funny! My brother's name is also my mom's maiden name, Easton." Ainsley sipped her tea and then inhaled sharply. "Speak of the devil; here he is!"

She jumped from her chair as her brother entered the room. They embraced as Easton looked over her shoulder at his mom. He appeared emotional. Ainsley took his hand and led him over to their mom's bedside. She gave him an overview of what had happened today.

"Hayden, this is my brother, Easton. Easton, this is Mom's nurse Hayden, and she is taking wonderful care of Mom tonight. Hayden, maybe you can explain all the tubes and the monitor numbers on the screen to him. I can't keep it all straight anymore."

Hayden patiently explained everything to Easton, who nodded solemnly in understanding. He asked some pertinent questions and then sat next to his mom and told her he arrived here from Vancouver. Most families are reluctant to speak to an unconscious person, so Hayden was surprised by his action. Easton encouraged Ainsley to go home to her family and get some rest, which she gratefully agreed to.

"Will you be here tomorrow night, Hayden?" Ainsley smiled wearily as she put on her jacket.

"Yes, I am on for the next two nights after this." Hayden bid her a good night and wished her a good sleep.

After Ainsley left, Easton sat by his mom's bedside. Hayden offered him a recliner chair and blanket and encouraged him to rest as well. He was concerned that he would be in the way of her care, but Hayden said she could work around him.

"When I wash her up or turn her, then I will ask you to step out and take a break," she advised.

Later in the night, Hayden was changing some medication bags. Easton told her some stories about his mom and how she loved her huge garden in the summer. Hayden thought sadly of Lena, but she couldn't bring her name up, thinking that she might become emotional. So, she spoke of her mom's garden on the farm.

"Oh, where is your farm?" Easton asked.

"It is just outside of Willow Creek. Do you know where that is?"

"I do. Home of the famous 'Back to your Roots' summer event!" Easton chuckled. "We grew up just outside of Lethbridge on a farm, and Mom and Dad took us to it once," Easton shared.

"Yes, it is a fun event. I missed it this year." Hayden said regretfully. "Does your mom still live on the farm?"

"No. When I was in first-year university here in Calgary, my dad was dying of cancer. They gave up the farm and moved to the city. My best friend still lives in the area, so I get out there on occasion," Easton said with a note of sadness in his voice.

"I'm sorry to hear that. You or your sister did not want to take over the farm?" Hayden asked.

"Not at the time. I wanted to pursue my school and then my business career. Farming is a ton of work."

Hayden thought of her dad and what would happen to their farm once he retired.

"My cousins took over the farm from us, but sadly they have not taken great care of the place. It is kind of a sore subject in our family." Easton looked over at his mom.

"I am so sorry," Hayden apologized. "I didn't mean to pry."

"It's all good, no worries." Easton smiled reassuringly.

Hayden had to change Coraleigh's abdominal dressing and asked Easton if he wanted to step out. He declined but moved back respectfully for his mom and for Hayden to have ample room to complete it.

Hayden changed the subject of the conversation. "So, how do you like living and working in Vancouver?"

"It's been great, but sometimes city life is not all it is cracked up to be. You know, astronomically expensive. But I love the ocean and all the great sites. And I love my job."

They chatted politely about Vancouver while Hayden changed the dressing. Once she was done, Easton went out for a break. Hayden washed Coraleigh up, changed her linens, and turned her with assistance from her colleagues. When Easton returned, Hayden dimmed the lights, and he slept in the recliner next to the bed.

Hayden kept busy, calculating the CRRT (dialysis) settings each hour. She monitored Coraleigh's vital signs and titrated her intravenous medications that supported her blood pressure. She suctioned her lungs through the endotracheal tube, and in the morning, drew off her morning laboratory blood tests.

The night shift soon ended. Hayden gave her report to the new oncoming day shift nurse named Helen. She was exhausted and headed to Clairese's to sleep. When she got home, Clairese was just coming home from her night shift too.

"Hey, Coyote. I have some exciting news for you! Remember that guy I was telling you about who is Simon's neighbor at his condo? You know, the attractive one with the nice car? Anyway, Simon told him about you, and we want to set you up on a blind date!" Clairese squealed and clapped.

Hayden groaned. "I don't know, Clairese."

"Come on, give him a chance! It could be a new beginning for you!"

She was too tired to argue. "Okay, I relent."

Clairese squealed again and hugged her. "I think December is going to be a new beginning for you!"

CHAPTER 26

Confidential Conversations

On Hayden's next shift, both Ainsley and Easton were at the bedside. Today, Coraleigh had another unstable day with her vital signs, and her medication regime had been changed.

"We are so glad to see you, Hayden!" Ainsley said, with a worried look on her face. "No disrespect, but Helen did not seem to have a very good grasp on things today."

They stepped out for a tea while Hayden completed her head-to-toe assessment. When they returned, they had brought her a tea.

"How thoughtful!" Hayden exclaimed. "Earl Grey is my favorite."

"I can't take credit for that. Easton saw your mug last night," Ainsley said, motioning to her brother. Easton nodded and smiled.

Hayden smiled back, then focused on calculating the dialysis numbers.

Easton's phone buzzed, and he frowned as he read the text.

"Please tell me that bimbo, Becca, is not contacting you still, Easton. Can she not take a hint?" Ainsley snapped at Easton.

Easton frowned at her. "We are just friends, Ainsley."

"Sure. She is a gold digger, ice queen, and she is *not* a genuine person." Ainsley rolled her eyes.

Easton put his phone away and sighed heavily.

"Why can't you meet a warm, kind, intelligent, 'salt of the earth' kinda gal?" Ainsley said more kindly. "Someone like Hayden, here."

Hayden looked up at them, and they all laughed together.

Ainsley left soon after, and the night shift progressed. Easton and Hayden again talked through the night. He asked her many intelligent questions about his mom's care. They often included Coraleigh in the conversation, even though she was heavily sedated and on a ventilator. Easton talked about his job in Vancouver. Hayden sensed he was very successful at what he did in business; he was intelligent, well-spoken, and well-dressed. Maybe Ainsley's comment about the 'friend' being a gold digger was not too far off.

Morning arrived, and Hayden's shift was over. Easton thanked her for her wonderful care. Coraleigh, fortunately, had a stable night, and her condition had improved.

Hayden was delighted to give report to Jonas this morning. She knew Jonas would take superb care of Coraleigh.

Hayden drove to Clairese's and sighed heavily. She so wished she were going home to her own place. As she drove up, she saw Clairese walking up the sidewalk with Simon. Simon must be working too, as he was in uniform, and the police cruiser was parked in front of the house.

"Hey, guys." Hayden greeted as she came in the front door.

They were standing in the living room, and both their expressions hinted that something was up.

"Simon is just finishing his shift but dropped by quickly to see us," Clairese said.

"Us?" Hayden smiled as she took off her coat.

"So, we are going to tell you something, but you can't repeat it, Hayden, or we will both get in trouble," Clairese warned her seriously.

Hayden suddenly felt very awake. "Of course, you know you can trust me implicitly."

"Last night, Lena's son Larry came into emergency. He had been badly assaulted," Clairese said solemnly.

"I arrested his creepy boyfriend, Jezz, at your old house. He is in jail," Simon added.

Hayden was shocked. "How do you know where I lived?" she asked Simon curiously.

They both exchanged glances, and then Clairese smiled shyly. "We have started to look for a house to buy together. We both love your old neighborhood, with the established trees and older homes. I pointed out Lena's place as we were driving around a few days ago."

Hayden nodded in understanding. She would never wish ill upon Larry, but she was relieved Jezz was in jail. "How bad is Larry injured?"

"He is admitted to the orthopedic floor as he has some fractures. He will recover," Clairese shared.

"Thank you for telling me. I promise I will keep it in confidence." Hayden assured them.

"On a lighter note…" Simon smiled and nodded to Clairese to continue.

"Yes, on a lighter note! Simon's neighbor Levi would like to take you to the Calgary Flames game on Thursday night for your blind date! Does that work?" Clairese squeezed her hands together in anticipation.

Hayden smiled at them both. "Yes, that works. Thank you for thinking of me."

Hayden headed off to bed after this but had trouble falling asleep. She was thinking of Larry, Jezz, and her upcoming blind date with Levi. But the last person she thought of, as she drifted off to sleep, was Easton.

CHAPTER 27

A Fine Line

Hayden slept amazingly well and awoke refreshed and ready for her last night shift, her 'pleasure' shift, as her dad would call it. She texted her mom and then got up and had a shower. She and Clairese had 'breakfast' together and packed their lunches for their shifts.

"Listen, I found out last night that I was able to trade a shift, so Simon and I are going to be away at his parents' home for the next six days to have an early Christmas celebration. We are going to take Buzz. His mom loves cats." Clairese laughed. "So, you will have the place to yourself! If you want to have Finnegan here, that would be fine. And of course, if your date with Levi goes well tomorrow night, then you are fine to have him over, too." Clairese winked at her.

Hayden rolled her eyes at Clairese but then thanked her. "That might work out. My mom and dad are bringing Paddy into Calgary for a doctor's appointment and could bring Finnegan by. I really miss him."

When Hayden got to work, she was happy to see Alana in the locker room; she had been working the day shift. "Oh, I miss working with you!" she exclaimed as she hugged Alana.

"Me too!" Alana said. "Hey, I see you are looking after Mrs. McCabe. Some of the girls are calling the son, 'Mr. McBabe'. He is so attractive! Too bad he is taken."

Hayden laughed and agreed. "The family are so nice and are both so attentive to their mom."

"I don't think the sister likes her brother's girlfriend, though. Some flowers were delivered here today from the girlfriend. She obviously doesn't know ICU can't accept flowers. Anyway, the sister was ranting to him about it. The flowers are now in our staff lounge." Alana chuckled. "Anyway, so good to see you Hayden, I've got to get back to my patient!"

As Hayden headed into the staff room, she saw Easton in the hallway with his back to her, speaking on his cell phone.

"Becca, my mom is in *critical condition* right now, so I can't come back to Vancouver for this event. I appreciate you sending the flowers, but you don't seem to get it."

Hayden kept walking into the staff room. She put her lunch away, verified that she had the same patient assignment, and then headed into the ICU to Mrs. McCabe's bedside. Jonas came out of the room after adjusting an IV pump and gave Hayden the report for the day. Coraleigh's condition had improved during the day, and she was off the dialysis. She still was requiring a small amount of intravenous medication to support her blood pressure.

Both Ainsley and Easton stayed at the bedside for the next couple of hours. Hayden enjoyed talking to them as she cared for their mom.

"We will miss you on your days off, Hayden. Do you have anything exciting planned?" Ainsley asked.

"Well, I am going to the Calgary Flames hockey game tomorrow night," Hayden responded as she straightened the IV lines.

"Ah, you are a hockey fan!" Easton smiled.

"Actually, no, it is a blind date," Hayden smiled coyly. Easton and Ainsley nodded and smiled.

Ainsley left at 10:00 p.m., and Easton took over the 'night shift vigil.' Ainsley stayed during the day and Easton at night.

Easton and Hayden repeated the night shift with light conversation as Hayden worked, and Easton sat at his mom's bedside. Tonight, they talked about the desire to travel, their shared love of Chinese food, and how much they both adored dogs. Hayden told him about Finnegan but left out how she 'obtained custody' of him; she felt that was too personal to share.

Easton told her a story about his mom and her mini-business of making hot packs out of flax seed and how successful she was. She sold them at craft fairs in the cities.

"Those sound like they would be a great thing to have, to help relax your muscles after a long shift," Hayden chuckled as she administered Coraleigh's antibiotics.

"I can send you her website to check them out," Easton offered.

As he texted the website to Hayden's phone, her heart went in her throat. *This is probably crossing the patient-caregiver professional boundaries*. It was too late now, as she felt her phone buzz in the pocket of her scrubs.

The night shift was almost over. Easton was dozing in the recliner chair, next to his mom, holding her hand. Hayden gave report to Jonas, and as she got up to leave, Easton opened his eyes.

“Enjoy your Flames game,” he smiled.

CHAPTER 28

Levi

Hayden did not sleep as well today. Her stomach churned with anxiety thinking about the message sent to her phone by a patient's family. She truly thought it was harmless, but she was disappointed in herself for allowing it to happen.

Her mom, dad, and Paddy arrived at 3:00 p.m and brought Finnegan. Clairese and Simon had already left on their trip. Finnegan was so happy to see her. She had a nice visit with her family, and then they had to get back on the road while it was still light out. Hayden decided to take Finnegan for a quick walk around Clairese's neighborhood. She missed her walks along the riverbank path by Lena's place.

The sun was still shining, but the wind was brisk, so it was only a short walk. Hayden showered and got ready for her date. He was picking her up at 6:15 p.m. Usually, she would arrange to meet somewhere for a first date, but with Simon being a police officer, she felt a bit safer that Levi would not turn out to be a psycho.

Promptly at 6:15, Levi knocked on the door. Clairese was right—he was very handsome and was driving a sporty Audi. He opened the car door for her, and they headed to the Saddledome for the hockey game. The conversation was light and easy, with only the occasional awkward pause.

"Would you like a drink?" Levi offered once they were seated at the game.

"I am post-night shift, so just a coke would be great," she smiled. Levi purchased two large cokes from the vendor and some popcorn. The hockey game was exciting and fast-paced. It was quite loud, so they didn't have much opportunity to chat while the game took place. During the breaks between periods of the game, they did talk, and he asked about her nursing job. She thought back to how Jean Marc would have just talked about himself on a date. How refreshing this was!

After the game, he suggested they go for a bite to eat. Hayden agreed that would be great. Wordlessly, Levi had taken her hand as they walked through the parking lot. Her stomach was nervous with excitement; this definitely was turning out to be an enjoyable date.

I think December is going to be a new beginning for you! Clairese's words echoed in her head.

"Any suggestions?" Levi asked.

"Well, I've heard about this great little pub in Kensington. It is supposed to have great food and a fun vibe," Hayden suggested.

She thought she saw a flicker of something cross his face, but she could have been reading into it.

"Sure," he agreed and nodded with a smile.

When they entered the pub, it was almost full. It had a fun atmosphere with darts, some pool tables, and good music. They found an empty table and sat down. Levi appeared a bit uncomfortable as he looked around, but then he turned to Hayden and smiled. The waitress came over and took their order.

Hayden needed something to calm her nerves. She ordered a vodka and soda with lime juice. Levi ordered another coke. She was impressed that he chose not to drink since he was driving.

She asked Levi about his job. He worked as a computer technologist at a large and upcoming company. He outlined his responsibilities, which sounded very technical but quite interesting. Then, their food arrived.

Hayden suddenly realized she was starved. She put her napkin in her lap and picked up her fork. Levi reached across the table and took her hand.

"Would you mind if we prayed?" he lifted his eyebrows.

Hayden was shocked but agreed. She took his lead and bowed her head. She felt surreal as everyone around them was laughing and kibitzing, the music was bumping, and they were praying. His prayer was about forty-five seconds long, but it felt like an hour.

They lifted their heads, and Levi dove into his meal. Hayden was still a bit shocked but carried on. She suddenly struggled for something to say.

"So, what is the significance of your name, Levi?" she asked brightly.

"It is a biblical name. I am named after Leviticus," he answered and then proceeded to tell her about who Leviticus was from the Old Testament in the bible and his significance.

Hayden thought of herself as spiritual and believed in God but was not an active church attender. She never judged others for their religious beliefs, but she suddenly felt uncomfortable. *Sinful?*

Levi put his fork down and grabbed Hayden's hand again. "Is Jesus Christ part of your life, Hayden?" Levi proceeded to tell her about his religion and his strict dedication to it. "Establishments like this, alcohol, and similar sins are not part of my life. But I can let this go tonight." Levi smiled and winked at her.

Hayden's appetite was gone.

Levi finished his meal, he paid, and they headed back to his car.

"I really need to get back to my little dog," Hayden forced a smile.

Levi drove her home. "I had a good time tonight, Hayden. I would really like to see you again." He started to lean closer to her.

Hayden could smell the garlic on his breath from his meal. Regardless, she did not want to kiss him or encourage him in the least.

"I had a nice time too, Levi, but I don't think we are compatible for a second date. Thank you for tonight, though," Hayden said softly with a sad smile.

Levi looked disappointed. "Okay, I understand."

As Hayden got out of the car, Levi turned to her and said, "I will say a prayer for you, Hayden."

CHAPTER 29

A Winter Walk

The next morning, she looked at her phone, and there was a text from Clairese:

How was the date?!

She answered, but it was short and to the point:

Interesting...

After breakfast, she bundled up and drove to her old walking spot along the riverbank by Lena's house. She contemplated driving past the house but couldn't bring herself to do it. She had brought a thermos of hot tea, and she and Finnegan went for a long walk. The sun was glorious, and the Chinook winds had blown in warm temperatures. It was Friday, and there were lots of people out on the path, maybe taking an extra-long weekend before all the craziness of Christmas.

After walking a fair distance, she and Finnegan turned to make their way back. Along the walking path, they approached a familiar park bench. Hayden had sat here after she and Jean Marc had broken up. She sat down with Finnegan on her lap and enjoyed the sun. She watched people walking past on the path or playing in the adjacent field. Finnegan barked as he saw two black lab dogs frolicking in what was left of the snow. There were two children, laughing gleefully with them and throwing snow. Hayden heard their father warn them, "Don't throw snow at them guys!" Hayden put her hand up to shade her eyes as she squinted in the sun. She thought she recognized the voice.

"Easton?" she called.

The man looked over at her and stared. "Hayden?" he replied, then laughed and walked towards her. He called Emery and Callen over.

"This is a coincidence!" Hayden laughed, and then with a more serious tone she asked, "How is your mom?"

"She is good today! She is off the blood pressure medication, and they are going to try and wean her off the breathing machine tomorrow. I slept at Ainsley's last night, after midnight. Ainsley is at the hospital now, so I thought I would give Kip a break and take my niece and nephew and the dogs out to burn off some energy. Is this Finnegan?" He leaned over and scratched Finnegan's ear.

"Yes, it is. I used to live near here, and this was our favorite walking path." Hayden smiled. "I am so glad your mom is doing better."

"Yeah, me, too! I might be heading back to Vancouver for a bit and then come back." Easton smiled. "How was the game last night?"

"Game was great, date not so much." Hayden smiled grimly.

"Ah, I'm sorry." Easton tilted his head to the side in empathy. He hesitated, like he was going to say something more, then called to the kids. "I've got to get these monkeys back home. They just live a few blocks over from here."

"Well, this was quite the coincidence! I am back to the hospital the day after tomorrow, so will probably see you then."

"You bet!" Easton nodded and waved as he herded the kids and dogs. Hayden watched as he lifted the little girl and put her on his shoulders. A wave of sadness suddenly came over her.

"Come on, Finn, let's go back to Clairese's."

CHAPTER 30

Overtime and Improvement

That evening, she spent most of the night on her phone. She spoke to Clairese and told her all the details of the date with Levi. She spoke to her mom about Christmas plans, and then she spoke to Shelby as well.

"You missed our Christmas party, so we definitely want to see you over the holidays," Shelby implored. "Chunk and Gena were sorry they missed you, too. Chunk wanted to talk to you in person."

Hayden was happy to hear he was doing well. She was also happy that the Montgomery family did not hold any ill will towards Chunk. Wyatt and Chunk had been lifelong best friends; they were like brothers.

When she got off the phone, she saw she had a voicemail from work. She listened and heard they were offering her an overtime day shift for tomorrow. She didn't hesitate to say yes, as she could use the extra money for Christmas gifts.

Is that really the reason why Hayden?

She phoned back and accepted the shift. Gabby, the nurse in charge tonight, was grateful. "They are really short-staffed for tomorrow."

When Hayden came in the following morning, the nurse clinician, Calvin, leaned over to her as he made up the assignment. Quietly, he asked, "Do you mind having Mrs. McCabe again? Her daughter requested you as the nurse. They were not happy with Helen or Danni's care."

I wonder why? Hayden thought cynically.

"No problem, Calvin," Hayden replied.

Inside, a little voice said: *Be careful, Hayden. Don't forget about the phone text.*

Ainsley looked so happy when Hayden sat down. Easton was not around. Danni was just coming out of Coraleigh's room. *What happens if Ainsley says something about Easton and me seeing each other at the park?* Danni would be the *first* person to read into it and report her, saying that sounded inappropriate!

Hayden jumped up and closed the sliding glass door. "Just closing this for report," she advised her professionally. Ainsley nodded from inside the room.

Danni gave her a jumbled, half-assed report and then left as soon as she could. Hayden was relieved. *Why am I so paranoid? I have not done anything wrong, she thought.*

Coraleigh's condition had vastly improved, just as Easton had said. She was off all of her medications to support her blood pressure and they had 'lightened' up on her sedation. She was now squeezing her hand to commands.

Easton soon appeared with sandwiches for himself and Ainsley. Just as they had the other night, they sat and talked with Hayden while she worked and cared for Coraleigh. They laughed and told stories to Hayden about growing up with Coraleigh as their mom. Hayden could see that Coraleigh might be listening as her closed eyes occasionally fluttered or she moved her arms. Hayden's understanding was that they were going to discontinue all the sedation on Coraleigh tomorrow in hopes of waking her up and weaning her off the ventilator.

Hayden was secretly disappointed when both Easton and Ainsley left to return home for dinner. She genuinely enjoyed their company, and she thought it was good for Coraleigh to hear their voices as well.

Hayden was back on regular duty the next two days, and Coraleigh was her patient again. Easton had returned to Vancouver for a few days to clear up some business before the Christmas holidays. Hayden and Ainsley spent the first part of the day mostly talking about Christmas. Hayden had transferred Coraleigh up in a recliner chair; she was drowsy but off all of her sedation. Tomorrow, they would start weaning her off the ventilator.

The following day, Coraleigh was successfully extubated and placed on an oxygen mask. She was making remarkable strides in her recovery. Ainsley was at her bedside during the day, encouraging her and assisting in her care as much as she could. Coraleigh wasn't speaking much since the breathing tube was removed, but she certainly was breathing well.

Hayden had the next two days off. Next week was Christmas! She elected not to attend the staff Christmas party, which was tonight. She was not into socializing right now.

Hayden spent her two days off looking again at potential apartments, which proved to be a waste of time. She felt disillusioned and frustrated. After her second day of fruitless searching, she went home and cried.

That evening, as she was getting ready for bed, she received a text:

Mom moved out of ICU today and is on the surgical floor. We wanted to thank you for all your wonderful care! Easton (and Ainsley).

The text brightened up her night. She hesitated but then elected not to respond to the text, to keep those professional boundaries in place.

CHAPTER 31

Chinese Food

On her next stretch of work, Hayden worked an easy day shift in CCU. There were not a lot of patients, and it was a good day. She only had one more day of work, and then she and Finnegan were heading home to celebrate Christmas with her family. The arrangement worked out perfectly. She was leaving just as Clairese (and Simon) were coming home from their early Christmas in Saskatchewan. Hayden had all her things packed, including all her family's wrapped presents.

At the end of her shift, Hayden got off the elevator and was heading towards the front door of the hospital. The front entrance had a sparkling Christmas tree in the front lobby, and there were a few other festive decorations for the season hanging as well. She admired them as she walked out and saw Easton standing there, talking on his cell phone. She smiled politely and waved, but then he put his hand up, indicating for Hayden to wait. She respectfully stayed back to allow privacy for his conversation, which he quickly ended.

"Hi, Hayden." he smiled. "I was just talking to Ainsley and giving her the update on Mom. Ainsley is at her daughter's preschool Christmas concert tonight. I got back here from Vancouver this morning, so I have been here all day with Mom."

Hayden nodded. "How is your mom doing? She made such a remarkable recovery in ICU!" she marveled.

"Yeah, she is a trooper! We are amazed and so grateful," Easton said with sincerity. "Listen, I wanted to thank you again for your wonderful care of Mom. We sent you a text, but I wanted to make sure you received it?"

"Yes, I did receive it, thank you." *I might be jeopardizing my career having given you my cell number,* Hayden thought uneasily. "It was a pleasure to look after Coraleigh."

"Well, listen, I know you just worked all day, so I will let you go," Easton said as they both proceeded to the front door of the hospital. "I'm just going to grab a bite to eat, maybe some Chinese. I am done with eating the cafeteria food!"

Hayden looked around nervously. She didn't want anyone she knew passing by to get any wrong ideas about them walking out the door next to each other.

Easton must have sensed this. "Oh, look, I'm sorry if I am making you uncomfortable."

They were standing outside now, and big snowflakes were lazily drifting down.

Hayden shrugged and chuckled. "No worries. Hey, if you need a good recommendation, there is a fabulous little hole in the wall, just down on Parkdale Boulevard. They have fabulous food."

"Sounds great!" Easton then hesitated. "Um, would you like to join me? It would be my treat in gratitude of Mom's care."

Hayden again looked around. Then she thought, *take a chance*!

"Here's the deal. It can't be in gratitude, or that crosses professional boundaries for me. How about it's just two hungry people after a long day, sharing some chicken fried rice?" she suggested.

"Deal!" he agreed.

Hayden gave him directions, and they agreed to meet there. Hayden first popped home to let Finnegan out to pee and gave him an extra treat. Her stomach was in butterflies; she *knew* that this was now crossing professional boundaries. However, she genuinely enjoyed Easton's company, and Coraleigh was not her patient anymore.

The restaurant was nearly empty when Hayden arrived, and she instantly relaxed. They sat in a little booth next to a window. They each ordered their favorite dish to share and individual bowls of wonton soup.

Conversation came easily—it was like they were old friends. Initially, the conversation was very superficial, but then it became more personal.

"What are your plans for the holidays?" Easton asked.

"I am going home to the farm tomorrow for an early Christmas. It is my turn to work the Christmas holidays, and then I will have New Year's off. I imagine you will be here for Christmas, or will you be in Vancouver?" Hayden said as she sipped her green tea.

"I've taken a leave of absence from work until my mom is out of the hospital. So, I will be here in Calgary. I am staying at Kip and Ainsley's. They have a good-sized house down by the park, near where we ran into each other." Easton smiled and nodded at the recollection.

Easton asked what her family Christmas traditions were. Hayden told him about their customary card game on Christmas Eve, and their family walks on Christmas afternoon, even when the temperatures were cold.

"Are you allowed to open any gifts on Christmas Eve? We are permitted to open one in our family." Hayden laughed.

"Absolutely not!" Easton teased. "No gift-opening until Christmas morning!"

Easton talked about looking forward to watching his niece and nephew opening their gifts Christmas morning and how he will miss his mom's cooking on Christmas day. "Don't get me wrong, Ainsley is a wonderful cook, but my mom has a special touch!"

Easton poured them both some more green tea. "Do you have exciting plans for New Year's Eve?"

"Not really," Hayden said, looking down at her dinner. Surprising herself, she then shared her breakup with Jean Marc in August and the whole Lena story with Easton. "I have not been in the celebratory kind of spirit to make plans for it."

"That sounds like a rough few months, Hayden. I can identify," Easton said sincerely.

Hayden then shared how she was living at Clairese's until January.

"You know, Kip and Ainsley own three properties here in the city. They are currently renovating one after a bad tenant trashed it. They might be able to put you in touch with a good place. I will text you Kip's business number if you want?"

"That would be great!" Hayden agreed. "I am getting worried about finding a place for Finnegan and me."

"I can imagine. I have thought about investing in a place back here again. I love Vancouver and my job, but I miss family. Especially now with Mom being sick." This time it was Easton's turn to stare into his food.

Hayden was not sure what to say. "So, what are your plans for New Year's?"

Easton told her about his best friend Ryan and his girlfriend Carleen. "We were hoping to get together. They are a great couple. I just wish we got to see each other more."

Just then, the waitress came over with fortune cookies.

"I'm sorry, but we are closing soon. Could we settle the bill?"

Easton paid the waitress, despite Hayden's objection. Hayden opened her fortune cookie.

A lifetime friend shall soon be made.

Easton opened his.

You will have many loves in your life but only one true love.

They both laughed awkwardly. Gathering their coats, they headed to the door and out to a new blanket of snow on the sidewalks and their cars.

They stood in the parking lot, under the twinkling Christmas lights of the restaurant. Huge snowflakes continued to fall silently.

Easton said, "I really had fun with you tonight, Hayden. A nice relaxing time is just what I needed."

They stood face to face, and then he smiled and shrugged. "If this is not too awkward for you and it does not cross your work boundaries, maybe we could do it again when I am here?"

Hayden replied, "I would like that, Easton."

CHAPTER 32

Christmas in Willow Creek

Even though it was late when she got home, Hayden felt bad for Finnegan, so took him for a run around the block in the dark. Later as she lay in bed that night, she anticipated she would not sleep. Her mind was racing, thinking of Easton, professional boundaries, her drive home tomorrow, Christmas with her family. She also thought of Louise and how sad her Christmas would be this year.

Surprisingly, she slept heavily until her alarm went off. She had a quick shower, tea and toast and then packed her vehicle. She was about to grab Finnegan to leave but decided to check her phone before the drive. There was a text from Easton. Her heart went in her throat, mostly because she was excited to hear from him, but also because she knew her contact with him was still possibly crossing those boundaries.

Thanks again for the company at dinner last night. It was a fun evening! Have a safe trip home. ☺ Easton

This time, she decided to reply. She took a deep breath as she texted.

I had a great time too! I will be back in Calgary in four days. Sending your mom healing wishes! ☺ H.

She closed her eyes and pushed send. She knew it was so unlikely, but she only signed her initial in case someone was reading Easton's phone. Grabbing Finnegan, she got on the road to head back to the farm.

As she drove, she glanced over at the fields. The blankets of snow sparkled from the sun's reflection on them. Some of the scattered evergreen boughs drooped with all the heavy snow on them. Hayden was grateful that the highways had all been ploughed.

When she pulled into the family farmyard, she saw that her dad had put up the Christmas lights on the house, and her mom had a fresh wreath hanging on the front door. There was a festive garland of greenery draped over the front porch. Hayden sighed to herself. *It was good to be home.*

Christmas with her family was a wonderful event, even if they did celebrate it a few days early. Winnie had been baking up a storm and there was an abundance of food. Despite that, it was tradition for her mom and her to bake some shortbread together, which they did that afternoon. The sweet buttery smell enveloped the kitchen, and Hayden savored it.

Later that evening, she and Paddy made their homemade nuts and bolts with various cereals and pretzels. Hayden loved this tradition with her brother, and his smile evidenced he did, too. Together, they bagged up the savory snacks in little bags with ribbon to give out to friends and family over the holiday season.

The next day, Hayden's family treated as Christmas Eve. In the morning, Hayden sat by the decorated tree, admiring all the decorations. Finnegan was curled up next to her, and she sipped on a cup of tea. One of the decorations was a bulb with her and Wyatt's picture on it from their first Christmas together. She stared at it, reflecting on how young and happy they were. The opening of a door interrupted her thoughts.

Her dad came in from the back porch with red cheeks, and his eyebrows were white with frost. "It is damn cold out there today!"

Hayden built a fire in the fireplace, and they all had a relaxing day, sitting around the crackling warmth. After dinner, they ended the day with their traditional family game of cards. As they opened their traditional one gift under the tree just before bed, Hayden thought of her conversation with Easton and their Chinese meal together. That familiar pang of guilt twisted in her stomach. *Professional boundaries!* She felt so agonized. She wanted to spend time with him again but knew it could be perceived as inappropriate since his mom had been her patient. She felt she couldn't share her concern with anyone.

The next day was their designated Christmas day. In the morning, they opened their gifts, followed by a delicious brunch. Hayden assisted her mom in getting the turkey in the oven, and then they all bundled up for their walk down the road. Finnegan stayed behind, but Butch ambled along with them all. It was brisk, so it was shortened to only a twenty-minute jaunt. Christmas dinner followed late in the afternoon, and Hayden felt like she would not need to eat for another week.

The day before she left back to Calgary, she went over to Shelby and Dean's. The twins were so cute and interactive, and Hayden loved playing with them as they crawled on the carpet. They all had a fabulous visit.

As she was about to leave, Shelby apologized. "Chunk had said he was going to drop by. I am not sure what happened. Dean texted him, but he hasn't answered." She shrugged her shoulders.

"No worries, Shelb. I need to head back to my parents. I want to have an early start tomorrow, roads and weather permitting." Hayden hugged Shelby goodbye and headed outside, bracing herself for the cold.

As Hayden approached her car, she heard someone call her name. She looked up to see Chunk getting out of his car and waving.

"Hi, Dylan." she greeted, making sure she respected his request for the name. He walked over to where she was standing on the sidewalk, and they stood facing each other. This time, it seemed a little less awkward.

"I'm sorry, Hayden, I meant to get over here sooner. I have misplaced my cellphone and was looking for it. I think I left it in Gena's car."

Hayden smiled and nodded. Chunk had lost some weight, and some hair. He had cropped it short with the hair loss.

"You look good, Dylan. I am glad you are back on the right track, and I am especially happy to hear that you and Gena are back together." She put her mittened hand on his arm.

Chunk nodded wordlessly. Then to Hayden's surprise, his eyes filled with tears.

"I thought I was disrespecting Wyatt's memory by being such an idiot. I knew if he were still alive that he would kick my ass." He looked down and kicked some snow. "It just took me a bit of time to realize that."

Chunk looked up and wiped the tear on his cheek quickly. "How are you doing, Hayden? Do you have anyone in your life?"

Does she have anyone in her life, she thought? She had not heard from Easton since her text.

"No, not really," she shrugged.

"Wyatt loved you so much, and he would want you to be happy, Hayden." Chunk said softly.

This time, it was Hayden's eyes to fill with tears. "I know." she nodded. She shivered in the cold.

"I am so glad I got to see you, Hayden. Take care of yourself." Chunk leaned over, and they embraced.

"Bye, Chunk," Hayden said and turned and walked to her car.

CHAPTER 33

A Close Call

The next morning, Hayden headed back to Calgary and left Finnegan back with her family. She almost dreaded going back. She wanted her own space. The afterglow of the Christmas celebration was over, she had not heard from Easton again, she had no place to live yet, and she felt lonely, especially at work.

She arrived at Clairese's house at noon and put all her things in her room. Clairese arrived home at 3:30 p.m from an eight-hour shift. They sat down to have tea and catch up.

"You are welcome to join Simon and me for dinner. I am just going to whip up some pasta," Clairese invited.

Just then, Hayden's phone buzzed.

I have the information from Kip regarding some properties for rent. Are you up for a walk at that park and then maybe a bite to eat? I can tell you all about it. Easton ☺

Hayden jumped out of her chair.

"Thank you anyway, Clairese!" and she went back to her room, leaving Clairese looking at her skeptically.

Twenty minutes later, Hayden was bundled up and leaving. "I am going for a walk, and then I am going to grab something to eat. See you later!"

Hayden's heart was racing. Her stomach was alternating between butterflies and knots. *I don't care about the consequences right now,* she thought.

Hayden and Easton met at the park bench where they first ran into each other. Easton was waiting for her with a cup of hot chocolate and a big smile.

As she approached him, she admired his tall, athletic physique, short black hair, and then, when she reached him up close, his green eyes. He really was handsome. *Mr. McBabe!* She smiled at the memory of the conversation with Alana.

"How was your Christmas with your family?" he greeted her.

Hayden felt giddy when she saw him. She felt like she was cheating or something with these secret meetings.

Luckily, the temperature was a little warmer today, and there were able to sit outside for a while. They sat and drank their hot chocolates as she told Easton about her celebration. He told her that they anticipated his mom might be discharged home from the hospital for December 26th! Hayden said she was so happy to hear that.

"As I mentioned, I took a leave of absence from work until the New Year to spend more time here with my family." he turned and looked at her. For a split second, she saw something cross his eyes. *Did he want to say to spend time here with me, too*? Her heart flip-flopped at the possibility.

"I am working day shifts over Christmas, starting tomorrow the 23rd until the 26th. For us as nurses, if you work Christmas, then you have New Year's off," she explained. "Did your work give you a hard time, asking for all this time off over the holidays?" Hayden inquired.

Easton smiled. "No." Then he chuckled. "I'm the boss, so it's all good."

They were both getting cold, so they decided to walk. About five minutes into the walk, Easton took her hand and looked at her. "Is this okay?"

Hayden's heart did a triple flip. "Yes." She blushed in the cold.

After walking a distance, they decided to turn around and head back as they were both cold and it was getting dark already.

"Are you still up for a bite to eat?" Easton asked. "I can show you the information from Kip and Ainsley. I am going to head back up to see my mom this evening too."

"That would be great. I can't have a late night, either, since I work tomorrow," she agreed.

"Kip told me of a great little pub in Kensington with excellent food. Would that be okay with you?" Easton suggested.

Hayden almost burst out laughing. "That would be great!" she agreed. *Will we have to pray before eating*?

Easton and Hayden met over there, taking their separate vehicles. It was not as busy as the last time Hayden had been there, but the festive spirit was certainly present. Hayden nervously looked around for anyone that she knew from work when they entered. She wasn't sure if her stomach was hungry or nervous.

Easton chuckled after they ordered their meals. "My ex, Becca, would hate a place like this. She was into all the sophisticated scene-type places in Vancouver."

Hayden then shared the story of her date with Levi with Easton, and they both laughed.

"Some people are just not suited for each other," Easton surmised as he took a swig of his beer. He went on to explain how Becca had been convinced that she and Easton were suited to each other.

"We did have fun at events together, but she wants different things in life. We have stayed friends, but I am realizing that even that is not a good idea anymore."

Their food arrived, and they enjoyed their meals. Their conversation flowed easily. After they ate, Easton told her that Kip and Ainsley had a property available to rent.

"Does Ainsley know that you and I have met up a couple of times?" Hayden asked tentatively.

Easton's eyes sparkled. "Yes, she does. She has no problem with it if that is what you are asking."

Hayden sipped the last of her drink. "Seeing you still borders on crossing those professional boundaries. I don't want your family to be uncomfortable with it."

Easton put his hand on hers and then clasped her fingers. "I don't have a problem with it, do you?"

Hayden looked back into his green eyes. "No problem at all. I love spending time with you."

They stared at each other a moment, and both smiled. Then, Easton looked at his watch.

"I am so sorry, but I should head up to see my mom."

Hayden insisted on treating and paid the bill. As they left the restaurant, Easton hugged her and kissed her on the cheek.

"I will talk to you tomorrow, okay?" Easton headed up the street, and Hayden turned the other way to head to her car. Just as she turned the corner, she almost walked into Alana, Shaye, and two male companions.

"Hayden!" they yelled and hugged her.

"What are you doing here? Were you just at the Pub?" Shaye asked.

Hayden stammered and swallowed nervously. "Yes, I was grabbing a bite with a friend." *Did they see her with Easton?* Her heart was racing with anxiety.

"Who? Anyone we know?" Alana teased.

"No, nothing like that. Just an old friend." Hayden said.

The girls introduced their male friends to Hayden and then bid her goodnight.

That was a close one, thought Hayden as she made her way to her car.

CHAPTER 34

Dinner Decisions

When Hayden got home that evening, Clairese had already gone to bed. Hayden quietly packed her lunch and then headed to bed herself. Not surprisingly, she had trouble falling asleep.

Was she doing the wrong thing? Was the risk of seeing Easton worth losing her job? Would it come to that? He lived in Vancouver; was this just a short-term thing for him?

All these thoughts arose again when she awoke the next morning. She had to do her best to stay focused at work. Luckily, she had a postoperative patient that required her full attention. During her lunch break, Hayden read a text from Easton, asking her if she wanted to join him and the McCafferty family (Kip and Ainsley) for pizza after her shift.

"Hayden?" Danni interrupted her thoughts. "Your food in the microwave is ready, and I would like to put mine in," Danni said flatly, with her usual sullen face. She was standing next to the microwave, holding her frozen dinner.

"Oh, sorry," Hayden said, quickly pocketing her phone and jumping up. She felt like a child caught reading something that they were not supposed to.

After she grabbed her food, she texted him back: *That would be great!*

With directions from Easton, she drove over to the McCafferty home. It was a new build in an older area and was quite modern appearing. As Easton had stated, it was not far from the river walk where she walked Finnegan, and she had run into Easton. As she approached the house to knock, Hayden felt nauseous. What does Ainsley really think of her with Easton? She had been so vocal with Easton about Becca. Her answer came the minute she walked in the door. Wordlessly, Ainsley came over and hugged her warmly.

They shared a pizza dinner with Kip, Ainsley, and the kids, Callen and Emery. It was relaxed and casual, but Hayden still felt a bit nervous.

Emery insisted on sitting next to Hayden during dinner. After dinner, the kids came back into the living room in their pajamas to say good night to everyone. Emery came over to Hayden, who was sitting next to Easton on the couch.

"Are you going to be Uncle Easton's girlfriend now?" she asked innocently.

There was awkward laughter in the room.

"Emery, that is private and not polite to ask, Honey!" Ainsley chided Emery.

Emery gazed sadly back at her mom but then looked back at Hayden and whispered mischievously, "I hope so!" and then scampered off to bed.

After the kids went to bed, Kip and Ainsley told Hayden about the investment property they owned, that they were just finishing renovating. They owned three different properties. It's what Kip did for a living; he would buy homes, renovate and flip them. Sometimes, they kept them as investment properties to rent out. They outlined that this one was a very small two-bedroom house in an older neighborhood. Not as quaint as the neighborhood where Lena had lived, but it would only be a fifteen-minute commute to the hospital and had a small yard for Finnegan. They showed her some photos of the place, and it looked so perfect.

"I am not sure if I can afford to rent a house," Hayden said hesitantly.

"We would be grateful for a responsible tenant. I am sure we can work something out that would be reasonable for both of us," Kip outlined.

Hayden was worried. What happens if nothing becomes of her and Easton? Would that become awkward and uncomfortable? She decided again, *take a chance*!

She was excited at this possibility of having her own house to come home to again. In the summer, she could plant her own flowers. Hayden agreed, and they said she could have possession on January 1st, though they might have a few more repairs to complete after she moved in. They signed some papers, and the deal was done!

The four of them visited for another hour, mostly about Coraleigh and plans for her when she is discharged. They told Hayden they were all excited to have a late Christmas celebration with her when she was discharged from the hospital.

"Speaking of hospitals, I should be going since I work again tomorrow. I hope you all have a wonderful Christmas with the kids and Coraleigh." Hayden said sincerely. "I am so excited to move into my new place; that is the best Christmas gift ever! I can't thank you enough. Thanks for the pizza, too."

Kip and Ainsley said they were happy to have her as a tenant and saw her to the door.

Easton walked her out to her car. "I think this will be a great thing for you. It is a great property. Hopefully, I will be invited over on occasion?" he asked with a smile and his eyebrows raised.

"I think that could be arranged," she smiled shyly and then shivered in the cold.

Easton stepped forward closer to her.

"So, I am just going to throw something out here, completely out of left field. I am not sure what you have planned for New Years'. If my mom's recovery continues to go well, I was thinking of heading home to Vancouver for a New Year's event sponsored by my company. I was wondering if you would like to come with me?" he asked quickly and nervously.

Hayden's stomach flip-flopped.

Easton continued, "I have invited my friends Ryan and Carleen, and they are going to attend the event, too. They are staying at a nearby hotel."

Hayden was floored. They barely knew each other; they hadn't even kissed. Then she looked him straight in the eye.

"Where would I stay?" she asked meekly.

Easton put up his hands in defense. "I will be a perfect gentleman. I have a two-bedroom condo. But if you would feel more comfortable, I could arrange a room at the same hotel as Ryan and Carleen."

Hayden moved closer to Easton. "Yes, I would love to come and spend New Year's with you."

With that, Easton leaned down and kissed her, tentatively at first, then deeply.

Hayden was confident she had made the right decision.

CHAPTER 35

New Year's Eve and New Beginnings

When Hayden returned to Clairese's, she was still up, sitting in the kitchen. She looked at Hayden skeptically, with her arms folded.

"I am not your mother, but please tell me you are not secretly seeing Jean Marc again, Hayden."

Hayden chuckled. "No, I am not." she wanted to tell Clairese everything, but she just couldn't trust anyone at this point. "I just can't tell you anything right now."

"Are you seeing a married man?" Clairese asked incredulously.

"No, Clairese! I need to go to bed. I promise I will tell you as soon as I can."

Hayden's shifts over the holidays were steady. She still felt very nervous about the WHOLE situation—the professional boundaries, a possible relationship with Easton, this new house with Kip and Ainsley as her landlords—all of it could blow up in her face. Could she cope with that after these past few months?

She finished her last shift on December 27th. Easton had sent her multiple texts over the holidays with pictures of the kids, their dinner celebration, and today, a photo of Coraleigh relaxing at Ainsley's. She wasn't quite ready to go to her own home yet. Easton had invited Hayden over every night after her shift, but she felt it was important for them to have this private family time. But tonight, she went over to meet Coraleigh.

"Mom, this is Hayden, and she was one of your wonderful nurses while you were in the ICU. She was our *favorite* nurse for you, so much so now, she and Easton have become great friends!" Ainsley explained to her mom. Everyone, even Coraleigh, chuckled at the subtle hint in Ainsley's last words.

Critical care nurses don't always have the opportunity to meet their patients after they are discharged from hospital. Hayden was surprised at how emotional she felt after meeting Coraleigh. They had a lovely visit, getting to know each other. Coraleigh expressed her gratitude for the care she received in the hospital.

Hayden was not ready to have Easton come over to Clairese's, so he again walked Hayden out to her vehicle, but this time, he came and sat inside the car with her for a while. The windows fogged up during their passionate kissing session. "I feel like I am in high school again," Easton laughed.

Easton told her he made arrangements for their flights to Vancouver. He had already forewarned her about having a fancy outfit for the event.

"I am excited for you to meet Ryan and Carleen. I know you will like them, and we are going to have a great time! Ryan was my best friend growing up, and he and Carleen still live back in my old hometown."

Hayden did not tell anyone that she was going to Vancouver, not even her family. She felt a bit guilty, and she was vague with friends when they asked what her plans were. Clairese was still suspicious that she was seeing Jean Marc again. When she saw the suitcase come out, she was back to being convinced it was a married man.

On December 29th, Hayden drove over to the McCafferty's and left her vehicle there. She and Easton took an Uber to the airport. Easton had bought first-class tickets for the flight. She felt like a celebrity but also wondered about the cost.

"Remember, I invited you, so this is my treat." Easton winked and then kissed her lips. Butterflies fluttered inside her.

While they waited for the flight at the boarding gate, Hayden got up and went to the washroom. As she exited out of the washroom exit, she saw Gurpreet, one of the ICU unit clerks. She was standing in the main terminal hallway with some friends or family. She smiled and waved at Hayden. Hayden waved back and then felt her stomach knot. *Did she see me with Easton? She would easily know who he was.*

As she walked back to her seat, Easton looked up and smiled at her. Hayden melted and thought, *I don't care anymore if anyone finds out.*

The trip to Vancouver was spectacular. Easton's condo was in a high rise in Oak Bay, near the marina. It was furnished with a very masculine touch and quite sparse to Hayden's surprise. "I don't spend a lot of time here. I work too much," he joked.

He hadn't lied; there was a small guest room. She put her bags in there, and shortly after, Ryan and Carleen arrived. Easton was right; she loved them straight away. Carleen was warm, fun and they had lots of laughs. They became fast friends that first evening.

Hayden and Carleen went into the kitchen to pour themselves another glass of wine. Easton and Ryan had turned on a sports game and were cheering about something.

Carleen touched Hayden's arm. "I just want to tell you how much I like you, Hayden. I think you and Easton make a great couple," she smiled sincerely. Then she lowered her voice, "I am not sure if Easton has told you about his ex, Becca. She and I did not get along."

Hayden nodded, "He has told me a bit about her."

"Well, I have a great feeling about you two. Ryan and I will look forward to spending more time with you guys!"

After they had left for the evening, Easton and Hayden spent a couple of hours making out in her room. It was romantic and passionate, but they agreed not to rush anything and not be intimate yet.

The next day, the two couples toured around Vancouver together. It was overcast, cool and rainy, but they still had a great day. Hayden felt on cloud nine. Easton held her hand, was attentive, and was not afraid to show her any affection. Having Ryan and Carleen there was also insightful. It helped Hayden see Easton at his most relaxed with friends. That night, they had a fabulous seafood dinner at a restaurant near the pier.

Ryan and Carleen went back to their hotel. Easton and Hayden lay on the bed in Easton's room, which had a spectacular harbor view. Christmas lights sparkled off the water, and the moon was bright tonight. They ended up talking for a couple of hours about future goals in between kissing sessions until they fell asleep wrapped around each other.

New Year's Eve was the next night. When Hayden emerged from her room after getting ready, Easton was initially speechless. Her dress was black, fitted, and sparkly. She had put her hair up and wore sparkly, dangly earrings.

"You look spectacular!" Easton whispered huskily in her ear and kissed her neck.

A town car picked them up and then swung over to the hotel where Ryan and Carleen were staying. The event was at a boutique hotel. There was money and jewels everywhere. Hayden suddenly felt a bit out of place. Carleen confessed that she felt the same way. They walked over to a table to get glasses of prosecco.

"Red alert," Carleen whispered to Hayden. "Becca the bitch at your nine o'clock."

Hayden looked up discreetly and saw a tall, thin redhead in a bright blue sparkly long dress scrutinizing her from afar. Hayden looked away. She took a sip of her drink and looked back up to see Easton across the room, gazing adoringly back at her. He beckoned her to come over to meet someone. She took a deep breath and walked over. He put his hand on her back, and she instantly relaxed. When she looked back at Becca, it was *her* who turned away.

That night, as the confetti and streamers fell and the noisemakers squawked around them, it seemed like it was only Easton and Hayden in the room as they kissed in the New Year and a new beginning for them both.

CHAPTER 36

The New Year

After their New Year trip in Vancouver, Hayden moved into the little house with the help of Easton and Kip. The roads had not been great in Calgary the first week of January, so she didn't want to ask her dad or Paddy to help. The three of them drove down to the farm with Kip's truck and a U-Haul trailer.

Winnie had made them a delicious lunch of hot chicken soup and biscuits for their arrival and before they started loading things up. She introduced Kip and Easton as her 'friends' but that Kip was also her landlord. Her parents didn't say anything, but Hayden suspected they were confused by the arrangement. There was no stress about bringing the boyfriend home to meet the parents this time, as they were completely unsuspecting. Or so she thought.

Everything was loaded, and they were ready to head back to Calgary. They all popped back in the house to say their goodbyes to her mom, and to thank her for lunch. As Hayden hugged her mom goodbye, she whispered to Hayden.

"He is a wonderful young man. I would hang on to that one."

Hayden was going to protest and say they were just friends, but she was aware that her mom knew her daughter better than that.

Easton was still on leave of absence, so they spent three blissful weeks in the house together. Easton worked from her house when she was at work or when they both weren't over at Coraleigh's house helping her. Finnegan loved Easton and Hayden joked that he liked him better than her now!

After she moved into her house, Hayden finally confessed the situation to Clairese and how she had met Easton. She told her that she still worried about people's judgment once they found out, especially her manager. She wasn't sure if she could be reprimanded anymore.

"Oh my gosh, Hayden, I thought it was going to be a lot more scandalous than this! I wouldn't worry about it." Despite Clairese's reassurance, Hayden still did not share her relationship at work with anyone.

Easton headed back to work mid-January in Vancouver but was frequently back to Calgary on the weekends, and Hayden even went back out to Vancouver to visit him.

The day before Valentine's Day, Hayden was working the day shift in the ICU. She still felt a bit lonely without her friends, but she was more focused at work. That afternoon, she was sitting and charting on her patient when the unit clerk, Jana called her over to the desk. Jana was new on the unit and very friendly.

Jana handed Hayden a vase of a dozen red roses with a plastic overwrap.

"Oh, Jana, you might not know, but flowers are not accepted in the ICU for patients," Hayden informed her kindly.

Jana smiled. "Hayden, read the tag. They are for you!"

Suddenly, it was like everyone stopped what they were doing and stared in Hayden's direction. Hayden felt the flush creep up her cheeks. No one knew she was seeing anyone. She didn't tell anyone at work anything personal.

"Who are THOSE from Hayden?" she heard someone call out.

Hayden took the flowers to her workstation and opened the card.

Thank you for starting my year off perfectly! I can't wait to spend more of them with you!

Love, Easton

If she could get any redder, she did now. She was so flustered. She slipped the card in her pocket and asked Nancy, the nurse next to her, if she could listen for her patient's alarms while she moved the flowers to the staff lounge to avoid allergies for the patients.

As she walked past, Kelda, the new obnoxious nurse in their group, asked: "So are you going to tell us who those are from, Hayden?"

"Oh, it is just a friend," she lied.

"Sure," snorted Danni. "Maybe from someone in your past Hayden?"

Hayden ignored Danni's tasteless comment referring to Jean Marc and walked out of the ICU and then into the staff lounge. She set the vase of roses on a table farther back, so they wouldn't get knocked over. Then she quickly texted Easton that she received them and how amazing they were. She couldn't wait to see him after her shift.

As it turned out, the oncoming shift was some of her old group mates, Jonas, Alana, and Shaye. When they came into the unit, they started to tease her about the flowers.

"Who are they from, Hayden? Are you seeing someone new?" Alana and Shaye demanded, but Hayden stayed tightlipped.

When she got home, Easton had arrived back from Vancouver and had already walked Finnegan. He had ordered in Chinese food and had set her table with candles. It was so romantic!

That night after their Chinese feast, he had a big idea to talk with her about. Easton wondered if she would consider moving to Vancouver this summer for six months to a year and work there. They could keep renting the house here in Calgary as a base to return to frequently.

"I am hoping to partially move my business. The base would be in Vancouver, but I would be in Alberta. I am ready to come back home to Alberta, but I need a year to get that organized. I just don't want to be apart from you, Hayden."

Hayden's mind was whirling. They had only been together for a short time, and she worried about being away from her family. He told her that they had lots of time to think about it, but he wanted her to start considering it.

Hayden slept soundly in Easton's arms that night. She dreamed of the sparkling lights on the water in the harbor.

CHAPTER 37

A Surprise Trip

June, four months later

Easton, Hayden, Ryan, and Carleen sat around a breakfast table next to the beach, sipping mimosas. The tropical breeze gently blew, and they could hear the waves crashing into the beach from where they sat. They munched on fruit and small pastries while they laughed and talked.

"I tell you, I could get used to this every day," Ryan toasted his glass in the air, reclining in his chair. He had his sunglasses on and hat tipped down.

Carleen laughed. "We just bought a farm. I don't think we have the money there, handsome."

Ryan and Carleen had been looking for a farm for a while and Hayden put them in touch with Tate and June Montgomery. Since June's stroke and with Tate having no one to take over the farm since Wyatt died, they were looking for someone interested in helping on the farm and eventually purchasing it. Ryan purchased a small portion of their land, then he and Carleen bought a mobile home to live in on the land. Ryan now worked for Tate with the eventual plan that he will purchase it all. It had been a perfect match.

Hayden had told Easton about the money she had deposited on the trip and the deadline looming for her to lose her money. Easton suggested the four of them go. He said nothing to Ryan and Carleen about who the trip had been originally organized for. They changed the destination and Bronwyn found them a fantastic deal.

They all sipped their mimosas and relished their surroundings. This was their third day on the island.

Easton sat forward in his chair and looked at Hayden. She nodded.

"So, listen, guys. Hayden and I have not been completely honest with you regarding this trip, and we have a confession to make," Easton smiled.

Ryan lowered his sunglasses, and Carleen sat forward in her chair with a questioning look on her face.

"Of course, we wanted you both to come and have an awesome time with us, but we also wanted you here to be our witnesses. We are getting married tomorrow."

Ryan jumped out of his chair and hugged his friend. "You lying son of a gun!" Then he came over and hugged Hayden. "You two are perfect for each other!"

Carleen was shell-shocked, then squealed and got up and hugged them both. "This is so exciting! I am so happy for you both!"

That night, Hayden slept in the room with Carleen and Ryan in the room with Easton. Ryan threatened to get Easton very drunk since they couldn't have a bachelor party.

Hayden woke up the next morning, before Carleen. *I'm getting married today.* It was surreal.

On Easter weekend, Easton had flown in from Vancouver on the Thursday to surprise her. He asked her to meet him at their bench, saying he had to walk Ainsley's dogs, and would she join him with Finnegan? When she got there, there were no dogs, just a very nervous Easton.

When Hayden sat down on the bench and saw how nervous Easton was, her first thought was: *This is it. This is when the fairytale with Easton implodes, and he breaks up with me.*

Easton took her hands in his and took a deep breath.

"I know this is crazy, we have only been together for a short time, but I feel like it is a lifetime. I know I want to spend the rest of my life with you. I promise to be faithful, committed to only you, and try and make you the happiest girl out there." With that, he presented her with an exquisite pear-shaped diamond, surrounded by two smaller round diamonds.

Hayden never hesitated and said yes. She couldn't believe it was happening.

That weekend, they drove out to Willow Creek. Hayden's parents had now met Easton several times and knew they were a couple but never realized how serious they were. They both really liked Easton but were very concerned when the four of them sat down together, and Easton asked for her hand in marriage. Although they never said anything, Hayden knew they thought she was pregnant. She assured them she wasn't.

"Hayden!" her mom said. "That did not cross our minds, but we are concerned that you hardly have known each other that long."

Hayden and Easton exchanged glances. "I know Mom and Dad. But we just know it is right."

They explained that the wedding was not planned yet. They also talked about how they planned to live in Vancouver for one year and then move to Willow Creek.

"We would like to build a house on the land here, Sir. I can run my business from home. I just need this year to organize that." Easton's suggestion was that they could eventually own the farm, allowing Ced, Winnie, and most of all, Paddy to live here as long as they wanted.

They planned the trip with Carleen and Ryan and the wedding thing just fell into place. Hayden felt a bit guilty that none of each of their family would be there, and Hayden also felt bad that Shelby would not be standing up with her. Easton and Hayden agreed that they would have a large (and surprise) celebration in Willow Creek in late June or July.

"I just want us to be married and be together all the time," Easton said to her one night as he held her. They were cuddled in her bed at the house that she was renting from Ainsley and Kip.

"Is there room out in Vancouver for Finnegan?" Hayden said with a sly smile.

"Absolutely!" he said, kissing her forehead and then scratching Finnegan's ears.

Hayden smiled and sighed as she lay there, recalling everything that had transpired in these few short months.

"Good morning to the bride!" Carleen said, snapping Hayden back in time for her wedding day.

Hayden showered, and Carleen styled her hair in a loose bun with a few strands of curls hanging down. She slipped on her white wedding dress. It was very simple—spaghetti straps, a jeweled belt, and mid-calf in length. She had on her sparkly earrings from New Year's, and then on her right hand, she wore Lena's ring.

She told me that she hoped and prayed that someday you would find true love, as she did with Uncle Henry. This ring symbolizes that love.

Carleen attached Hayden's veil to the bun in her hair. Hayden and Carleen's flower bouquets were delivered to the room. The two of them stood and looked at themselves in the mirror.

Carleen handed Hayden her bouquet and smiled. "You are such a beautiful bride, Hayden! I am so happy and honored to be here with you. Thank you for including us." Carleen looked at her watch. "Oh my gosh, we should start heading down to the beach; you don't want to leave your groom waiting!"

A light, fragrant, tropical breeze floated through the outdoor halls as they made their way down to the beach. They needed to walk past the pool area, and as they did, people smiled and nodded, and some even called out congratulations.

As they neared some stone steps leading down to the beach, they paused to let an elderly couple walk past slowly, followed by a young Mom towing a little girl, who was probably two.

"Come on, Sweetness, let's head to the pool!" the mom encouraged the little girl.

Hayden froze.

"Oh my gosh, isn't she cute!" Carleen gushed.

Hayden looked at the little girl with a mop of black curls and big brown eyes, wearing a ladybug-patterned swimsuit.

"What did you call her?" Hayden asked the Mom.

"Um, Sweetness?" the mom replied, looking confused at Hayden staring at her. "Wow, Sweetie, look at the pretty bride. Congratulations to you."

The little girl stared at Hayden. Then, her little face lit up into a big smile, and she waved her chubby little hand. "Bye-bye," she called as her mom carried her to the poolside, still smiling over her mom's shoulder.

"Hayden, are you okay?" Carleen asked in concern.

Hayden looked at her and nodded.

Carleen put her hand on Hayden's arm. "Are you ready to head down there and marry Easton?" she asked.

Hayden turned to Carleen and said with confidence, "I've never been more ready in my life to do anything else."

EPILOGUE

May, Three Years Later

Out in her yard on the farm, Hayden covered the 'forget me not' seeds with damp earth. She and her mom Winnie had been hard at work all morning, planting and cleaning the flowerbeds. Hayden's goal was to have her new garden abundantly full of the spring flowers and plants that both her mom and Lena had in their yard: bleeding hearts, tulips, daffodils, and crocuses. The 'forget me nots' would be a special summer tribute to Lena.

The garden was a project in progress. Hayden and Easton's house was finished being built in March. Their home was on the Barrett ranch, set further back, behind a grove of aspen trees. They were both so happy in their new space. Easton had planted some trees for her, including some flowering cherry trees, a weeping willow, and some lilac bushes.

After they were married, they moved to Vancouver for one year. Easton was able to have the year to adjust his business so that he could work from home in Willow Creek, with the occasional business trip to Vancouver. Winnie, Ced, and Paddy were thrilled to have them on the farm, and Easton did his best to also help Ced out on the ranch. Just back in April, he was up at 3:00 a.m; helping Ced deliver a calf with a heifer cow.

Coraleigh McCabe and the McCafferty family were regular visitors on the farm. Paddy relished in touring Emery and Callen around the farmyard. Coraleigh and Winnie got along like old friends, and it was often a bake fest when they got together.

Hayden looked at her watch. "Mom, I should probably head in and wash up. I need to leave soon to get to the airport in Calgary." Easton had been in Vancouver for three days on business. Hayden was going to pick him up at the airport, and then they planned to stay in Calgary overnight. Hayden had a doctor's appointment in the morning, and they also planned to visit with Coraleigh and the McCaffertys. Hayden also wanted to drop by to see Clairese and Simon and their new baby boy, Mitchell.

Two months after Hayden had moved into the house that she rented from Kip and Ainsley, Clairese had texted her:

Simon and I found and BOUGHT a house together! Check it out!

Clairese had attached a picture to the text. Hayden's eyes filled with tears when she recognized the house. It was Lena's. She knew Clairese and Simon had been looking in that neighborhood. She just never thought they would have the opportunity to buy Lena's. Clairese shared with Hayden later that they had to gut the inside of the house, as Larry (and Jezz) had not cared for it at all. She promised Hayden that she would care for all the plants in the yard, just as Lena had. Hayden was confident that she would.

Hayden cleaned herself up, changed, and grabbed her bag. As she headed out, her mom came over to hug her.

"Are you doing okay? I hope you didn't overdo it here in the yard." Winnie said, concerned.

"I'm good, Mom!" Hayden reassured her. "We'll be back in a few days. If you don't mind watering the newer plants, I would appreciate it."

Hayden drove down the gravel road, the dust billowing behind her truck. It was a beautiful spring day in Alberta, and the blue sky was filled with puffy white clouds. She sang along to the country music on the radio.

As she neared into town, she slowed and looked over at the large house and the sign in front: *Somewhere in Thyme*. The gravel parking lot in front was quite full of vehicles. Hayden smiled; she was happy that business was good. This was Gena and Carleen's tea house.

While in Vancouver one weekend, Carleen and Hayden had gone for 'high tea' one day at the *Pendray Inn and Tea House.* Carleen had been inspired to start something similar. She met Gena at Hayden and Easton's wedding celebration, and the two conspired and came up with the idea for Willow Creek. The play on the name of the teahouse came from a favorite movie of Gena's.

The tea house had wonderful food, including "Lena's fresh scones." Hayden had been so touched to see this on the menu at their grand opening. They had a small gift shop and, out back behind the teahouse, a huge greenhouse. Gena sold bedding plants in the spring, pumpkins in the fall and fresh wreaths and Christmas trees (that she had shipped in) in December.

Chunk and Gena had married in July, just months after Hayden and Easton. The following summer, Gena had given birth to a baby boy, whom they named, not surprisingly, Wyatt. Ryan and Carleen had married in the fall that same year. They had not had any children yet, but Hayden was sure that was in their long-term plan.

After their wedding in June, Hayden and Easton had returned to Calgary and Willow Creek to many surprised friends. Hayden was worried about what Shelby's reaction would be, that she had not been included in the surprise elopement.

"I knew you never wanted the big pomp and circumstance, Hayden. However, I would love to plan a big celebration here for you both!" Shelby said enthusiastically.

The party was held at the Willow Creek community center, and it was a great time. Hayden wore her dress and veil again, and it was a fabulous celebration. So much so that it motivated Shelby to start a business of her own.

Shelby and Dean built a beautiful new barn on the Montgomery farm and began a wedding and event business. Both Chunk and Gena and Ryan and Carleen had their weddings at the new barn. Shelby and Dean also expanded their business to include some 'Field to Fork' catering in the summer. Customers would dine at a huge table, out in the middle of a wheat field, all with homemade farm-fresh food, including June's different types of pickles.

Hayden marveled at how life comes full circle as she drove into the city. As she drove up Deerfoot Trail towards the airport, she saw the exit sign with the 'H' listed on it. She glanced over in the distance to see the rooftop of Memorial Hospital. It almost seemed like a lifetime ago that she worked there. After she and Easton had married and moved to Vancouver, she worked at Vancouver General in the Intensive Care Unit. While she enjoyed her time in Vancouver, she didn't love it and was so happy when their year was up, and they relocated back to Willow Creek. She was worried that Easton would miss living in Vancouver, but he genuinely loved Willow Creek. He reminded her that he grew up in the country and felt that he had the best of both worlds. "As long as I am with you, Hayden, I will be happy anywhere," he had told her. She smiled at the memory as she drove.

Hayden parked and headed inside the airport terminal. She had really missed Easton these last few days and couldn't wait to see him. As she stood outside his airport arrival gate, she thought about how happy they were together. They loved their life on the farm, spending time with both of their families and of course with all their friends.

The gate opened, and people started to trickle in from the arriving plane. Hayden could see Easton from a distance. She recognized his stride, and she could see the dark hair on his head, as he was so much taller than those around him. As he neared closer, they made eye contact, and he smiled. Even after three years of marriage, Hayden still melted when she saw his handsome face smiling at her. She drew in a deep breath, *her husband.*

"How is my girl?" Easton asked as he kissed her.

"I'm good," she answered and kissed him again. "I am happy you are back safe."

"How is my other girl?" he asked lovingly as he gently caressed her swollen belly.

"She is good, too," Hayden replied, smiling. Almost on cue, she felt the familiar kicks in her abdomen.

They headed over to the baggage carousel and waited.

"I have an extra bag," Easton laughed. "Several baby gifts were sent from the company." He recognized his suitcase and stepped forward to get his first bag.

Hayden's phone buzzed, and she looked down to read a text from Ainsley.

"Hayden?" a familiar voice asked.

Hayden looked up and was shocked to see Jean Marc standing in front of her. He was thinner, and his strawberry blond hair had tinges of grey at the temple. It was Jean Marc, but his swagger was missing. He looked empty.

"Jean Marc!" she exclaimed.

She was shocked to see him but was absolutely floored when right behind him, Louise stepped up, holding a baby, probably six months old.

"Hello, Hayden," Louise said, also visibly surprised. She looked at Hayden's obvious pregnancy. "Congratulations, when are you due?"

"Oh, in two weeks," she answered, with her hand on her belly.

There was an awkward pause as the three of them stood staring at each other in shock.

"This is our son, Elliot." Louise offered as she looked down lovingly at her baby. Elliot was of mixed race, with dark eyes and jet-black hair. "We adopted him three months ago."

"Well, congratulations," Hayden said sincerely.

Just then, Easton walked up. "This is my husband, Easton," Hayden said. "Easton, this is Jean Marc and Louise."

Easton's eyes flickered in recognition of the names, and he put his hand out. "Good to meet you both." Then he put his hand on Hayden's back. He knew this must be awkward for her.

"We are living in Montreal now," Jean Marc offered. "We have just travelled out here with Elliot to introduce him to Bernie's family. We still keep in touch."

Hayden nodded sadly. "That is lovely."

Elliot started to fuss.

"We should get going." Louise smiled. "Best of luck with your delivery, Hayden. I am happy for you."

With that, the two couples went their separate ways.

"Are you okay, Hayden? I am sure that was a bit of a shocker," Easton said, with his hand on her cheek.

Hayden smiled back at Easton. "I am good, Easton. Actually, seeing them puts me at peace."

As they walked out of the airport, hand in hand, Hayden took a deep breath. She looked up at her husband and laid her hand on her pregnant belly.

My heart is full.

ABOUT THE AUTHOR

Carolyn Vacey is a Registered Nurse in Calgary, Alberta, Canada, with thirty-five years' experience in Critical Care, Emergency and was a STARS Flight Nurse for twenty-five years.

She is married with three daughters. *Critical Prairie Hearts* is her first novel.

CRITICAL PRAIRIE HEARTS

Hayden Barrett is a critical care nurse living in Calgary who embarks on a risky romance. Intertwined in her life are some painful memories from her past, her challenging job, and her country roots. Will she find happiness?

Manufactured by Amazon.ca
Bolton, ON